WILLA'S
PURSUIT

T0007736

ALSO BY JAMES BASTIAN

Wisconsin Logging Camp, 1921

WILLA'S
PURSUIT

James Bastian

AN IMPRINT OF BOWER HOUSE
DENVER

This is a work of fiction. Names, characters, places, and incidents are products of the author's imagination or are used fictitiously and are not construed as real. Any resemblance to actual events, locales, organizations, or persons, living or dead, is entirely coincidental.

Willa's Pursuit. Copyright © 2023 by James Bastian. All rights reserved. No part of this book may be used or reproduced in any manner whatsoever without written permission except in the case of brief quotations embodied in critical articles and reviews. For information contact Conundrum Press.

BowerHouseBooks.com.

Printed in Canada
Cover photograph by scalinger, courtesy Adobe Stock
Internal photograph, courtesy iStock

Library of Congress Control Number: 2023930622
Paperback ISBN: 978-1-942280-68-2
Ebook ISBN: 978-1-942280-69-9

10 9 8 7 6 5 4 3 2 1

To Lindsay and Leah

Prologue

Several events, articles, studies, and stories influenced the writing of this book, including a 1926 account of three loggers in Rusk County, Wisconsin, who purported to have found a French explorer's petrified body in a hollow tree they cut down. However, an actual event, which took place in a parking lot in the City of Leicester, Great Britain, is particularly noteworthy. Archeologist Philippa Langley had a hunch that the body of King Richard III was not thrown into a river after he was killed in battle with the Tudors as legend had it. Instead, Langley and a few colleagues thought the body might have been buried at the site of the old Greyfriars Church, which was now under a sprawling parking lot. Acknowledging that the site was "a long shot at best," Langley described her first visit as follows: "The moment I walked onto that parking lot in Leicester, the hairs on the back of my neck stood up and something told me this was where we must look. A year later I revisited the same place, not believing what I had first felt. And this time I saw a roughly painted letter 'R' on the ground [for reserved parking obviously]. Believe it or not, it was almost directly under that 'R' that King Richard was found."

In addition to this account, there are documented xenoglossy* cases in which researchers report subjects becoming

---

*Xenoglossy: A putative paranormal phenomenon in which a person is able to speak or write a language he or she could not have acquired by natural means.

inexplicably fluent in a foreign language or acquired knowledge or memories of someone else who has long passed. There are countless episodes of ordinary people having extraordinary psychological experiences. Some of these include the sudden onset of delusions or nightmares, which result in a diagnosis that the subsequent interference with normal behavior is pathological, only to discover that the delusions have a basis in reality.

There are too many examples like these for the author to conclude anything other than ... the extraordinary happens.

1

The year 1971 was hell for me. I thought I was going crazy. There were inexplicable voices, visions, and dreams that turned my normal, predicable, and boring life upside down. The resulting stress, self-doubt, and challenges I had discerning reality from fantasy led the man I thought I would marry to dump me, ended my dream of becoming a psychologist, and sent me on a frantic search for the cause ... and hopefully the solution. I was desperate to end the tormenting delusions and dreams, and the subsequent depression, which was followed by bursts of manic and obsessive behavior.

I struggled trying to find answers to what was happening to me. Why do sudden onset delusions and obsessions occur? If a delusion is defined as maintaining a belief that experiences and thoughts are real despite overwhelming evidence that they are not, then what is the diagnosis if it ultimately turns out that despite the unlikely odds, the "delusions" are of real events? Just like the example that profs give in every Psych 101 class, "Are you paranoid if you constantly feel you're being watched and change your normal behavior to elude the pursuer, only to have it turn out you were being followed?"

I don't understand exactly what happened and I can't explain it. But it did happen, there is no denying that. Some people may believe I was just crazy, or it was a ghost, or that I was reincarnated. My best guess is that it was an acute psychotic episode or xenoglossy, but at this point knowing the label isn't important, only ridding myself of the night-mares is.

What I am certain of is that it began during my gradu-ate research project on sensory deprivation. Specifically, while I was submerged in the sensory deprivation tank, and it started immediately. After the first minute or two of the experience in the tank, I could no longer tell fantasy or ran-dom thoughts from reality. While it started during that in-duced psychotic state, eventually the visions took over my thoughts while I was awake, and dreams with recurring nightmares each night, which included infused information, even memories that weren't mine.

It started off normally enough. I remember it vividly. It was January 14, 1971, the first day of class of the second semester of my Ph.D. program at the University of Wisconsin in Madison. My project advisor and "special friend" started the first lab of our graduate research team consisting of me and two other doctorial students.

"Hi Doctor Janis."

"Good morning Ben, Willa, Alec. Please call me Dan. Has everyone read the 1957 article by Heron, and the others as-signed?" We all nodded. "Good. Next week please read Har-low 1951. That article and others by Doctor Harlow address the impact of deprivation of maternal contact in the social development of infant rhesus monkeys. While periphery to our research, Doctor Harlow is head of this department and keenly interested in this research. Consequently, you will become very familiar with his work before the end of your grad program. Ben and I got the tank filled and the water to ninety-four degrees. The sound suppressers, blinders, oxy-gen pump, and sensory suit are all tested. We're about ready to begin our first sensory deprivation experience.

"As you learned from the readings, in similar experi-ments students were only able to tolerate the sensory deprivation environment for short periods of time. Most terminated the experiment within ten minutes. Here is a sheet with the safety procedures we will follow on each

4

submersion. One of you will serve as a spotter, keeping an eye on the heart rate readouts and flow of oxygen, the other will watch the tank for signs of agitation and to operate the extraction hoist. Any questions on safety? ... Okay, any questions on the process?"

"Doctor Janis ... I mean Dan, why do subjects stay for such a short time? It seems like you could just take a nap and stay there for an hour or two. I'd love to have a place to nap where there are absolutely no distractions."

"Good question, Alec. The brain loses the ability to perceive time without physical cues. Previous subjects thought they were in the tank much longer than they were. Not by a couple of minutes but by a factor of five or more. In other words, if they were in the tank for five minutes, they thought they were in for twenty-five to thirty minutes or more."

"Are there any residual affects?" I asked.

"Yes, and they can be serious, Willa. Psychotic episodes, for example. The brain needs stimuli to operate normally. The differentiation between real and imagined thoughts and sensory perceptions require external stimulus. The absence of stimulus, which is what we will be doing, causes distress as the brain struggles to sort out what is real and what isn't. The entirety of the evolutionary process of the brain function of higher organisms has been based on receiving and interpreting both internal and external stimuli. Alec, to your point, the inability to use sensory cues to distinguish fantasy from reality can be disconcerting and likely also contributes to shorter duration submersions. This experiment is intended to monitor what happens when those external cues required by the brain are not present. There is a danger level here. As you might expect, you will be asked to sign a liability waiver acknowledging that you understand the potential dangers and you hold the university harmless."

"Yeah, we sure don't want the university to be responsible for screwing up a student. Have you been in the sensory deprivation tank, Dan?" Alec asked.

"No. If your findings are substantive, I may publish the

5

results so I will need to keep an independent, arms-length perspective. Your responsibilities are to refine the thesis and complete the data collection, while mine are to teach you about and review the literature regarding sensory deprivation, maintain experimental integrity, and ensure your data is valid and reliable. Any other questions? Okay, then let's get started. You'll each take a turn. Because personal tolerance levels vary, you will determine how long you stay in the tank. We will be able to hear you although you can't hear us. So you just have to tell us to extract you whenever you want out. Take it easy the first time. But if I detect significant agitation, I'll pull you out immediately. You'll have other chances. So, who wants to be first? Okay, Ben."

We each went to the restroom to change into swimsuits. I was the last one out. Alec whistled when I walked into the lab. I didn't say anything but based on his embarrassed sheepish look, the daggers I stared at him seemed to have the desired effect.

Ben stayed in the tank for eight minutes and forty-five seconds. Alec and I were eager to hear his description of the experience. It took Ben just a minute to strip off the wetsuit and other gear, but several more minutes to gather himself. He could not believe he was submerged for less than nine minutes, and like other subjects, he was certain that it had been at least an hour. After taking a couple of deep breaths, Ben told us how quickly he lost the ability to discern reality from the imaginary. This made the hallucinations and delusions, which began almost immediately, more frightening.

Despite Ben's account, Alec assured us he would outlast Ben and no doubt set a new collegiate record. He began flaying and cried out at just over seven minutes. Once extracted, he was noticeably shaking, pale, and clearly unnerved. He put his hand up when we asked him what it was like, and he walked out of the lab without a word.

My turn.

I put on my wetsuit and stepped each leg into the harness. The straps went under my crotch and held me front

6

and back like a mountain climbing harness. I watched Ben attach the clips from the harness straps to the cable to lift and lower me into and out of the tank. I climbed up the steps to the rim of the eight-footdeep vat filled with 94-degree water. Ben and Dan fitted on the helmet with blackened visor. The bulbous helmet fit over my entire head and fastened at my neck to the top of the wetsuit with snaps and a watertight flap over a zipper. Once fastened tight it was pitch black, and smelled like rubber and sweat. The pads at the top of the helmet fit snuggly around my head with headphones over my ears to block sound. The air intake hose was attached to a vent through the front near a microphone.

I said I was ready, but I was lying. I was really apprehensive. It felt like I was stepping off a ledge in the dark, with the promise that there was a net ready to catch me at the bottom.

The noise from the motor of the hoist and creaking pulleys was loud and clear when I was watching Ben and Alec being lowered, but was barely discernible, a distant hum at most from inside the helmet.

I felt the tugging of the cable until I was submerged. Once buoyant, I felt nothing and heard nothing in the blackness. Even the smells disappeared as I acclimated to them.

I tried to listen for the hum of the ventilator. What I thought might be a sound was just a faint ringing in my ears. Maybe I could hear my breathing, or if I blew or whistled. I tried both, but with the sound-abating headset I couldn't tell if I was just thinking about whistling or if I had actually tried.

Dancing lights seemed to appear.

Then ringing in my ears progressively grew louder. Like dozens of cathedral bells clanging in the distance. Then nearby. That's when the hallucinations began. I was transformed into a clapper in a bell and although completely stationary, I was certain that I could clearly feel myself swinging rhythmically and violently left to right. I decided to try concentrating on my meditation regimen, which I regularly use and is effective for me in reducing stress. Meditation began with my focus on a tingling sensation at the top of my head that I'd use as a cue to expand my suggestibility and completely relax. It always worked and was working now. I had done this so many times in the past that it was an automatic response, with the perception of a warm wave of relaxation starting at my forehead and slowly moving down my body. I usually repeated this process several times until I felt completely relaxed and refreshed.

I couldn't remain focused though. The tingling sensation that I used to trigger my relaxation process instead felt like spiders crawling on my head and down the sides of my face.

I tried to calm down and changed the relaxation cue to feeling weight in my feet. But I immediately felt as though I was sinking, accelerating like an anchor tied to my legs was pulling me deeper and deeper into an abyss. I could swear the water pressure on my body was rapidly increasing, crushing my chest. I was fighting for breath. "Get me out!"

2

Light pierced through an opening in my helmet. I thought I was dead. Off came the helmet. Deep breaths, eyes adjusting to the light, I was standing on the platform next to the tank.

"You got pretty agitated in there, Willa. When did you learn French?"

I was getting my bearings back. "What the hell are you talking about, Dan? I don't speak a word of any language other than English."

"You just shouted in perfect French, *faites-moi sortir!* 'Get me out!'"

"Bullshit."

"It's probably on the recorder, you shouted it loud enough. Ben, replay the tape."

"Willa, I heard it too. You said it plain as day. Here, listen."

Ben rewound the tape and hit play. It started with Dan's voice, "She's getting active, maybe thrashing" ... "*Faites-moi sortir!*"... "Extract her Ben, bring her up ..."

"Where the hell did that come from?"

"There must be some repressed exposure to French somewhere in your past. Do you have any French relatives?"

"Nope, they're all German, on both sides."

"Well, we pick up all kinds of extraneous information. You must have heard it somewhere and not given it a second thought until now."

"I suppose. By the way, how long was I in there?"

"Nine minutes, Willa, actually nine minutes and sixteen seconds."

Thank goodness we didn't have class again until Tuesday. I needed the five-day break before trying that again.

3

I've been dating Dan for six months. I couldn't believe he took me up on my suggestion that we have a coffee date last May. We first met when he was still a T.A. during my last semester as an undergraduate, a year ago. I didn't get up the courage to talk to him until I was accepted into the Ph.D. program. It was awkward at first because he was my thesis advisor and lab professor. We had only known each other casually from the two undergraduate classes he taught. Every girl taking psych classes loves Dr. Janis. He's good looking, charmingly awkward, with those wire rim glasses too small for his face, and is highly regarded professionally. A little short, I'm taller than him when I wear heels, but he's always perfectly groomed and wears a suit or sport coat to class even though most professors dress casually. He has a photographic memory, although he refers to it as "retrieval savant." He just flat out remembers everything he's ever read, I mean everything. Recites it verbatim. He impresses the hell out of his colleagues and his students and me. It's likely a big reason he did so well all the way through school, and why everyone seems to think he's so damn smart. Dan was a psychology department prodigy. Breezed through undergrad in two and a half years, MS and Ph.D. two years later. Colleagues defer to him, publications want his contributions, and professional organizations want him to speak at their dinners. He can be hard to read, sometimes coming off as aloof or too bookish, but I'm still infatuated with him.

I'm proud of him, too. I feel special when we're out, and admittedly maybe a little smug when coeds or women faculty flirt with him. When Dan and I started seeing each other, I felt like the luckiest girl on campus. Of all the women on campus, he asked me out—a self-conscious, tom-boyish, flat-chested, "hanging on by her fingernails" grad student. Dan tells me I'm pretty, but after being teased about my looks incessantly by my two older brothers as a kid, it's hard for me to feel that way. I know they were just being brothers, but they sure shot a hole in my self-esteem.

Dan's coming up north next month to meet my family. I can't wait to introduce him to my mom and dad. They will love him. Well, Mom will for sure, and I think Dad will be impressed, too. Dad thinks it's important to know what's going on in the world and Dan knows everything. I'll be curious to hear my dad's assessment. He has an uncanny ability to size up people.

Dan and I went out Saturday night, and I slept over at his apartment. Usually did. It wasn't as exciting as it was at first. I'm still attracted to the guy, but, I don't know, maybe we've just become an "old couple" after six months.

4

Ben, Alec, and I had to keep a journal of our experiences in the tank, make copies for each other, and turn one in to Dan each week. Dan intends to include the journal entries and data we collect with other research for publication.

Alec's account of his experience was funny, although not to him. In his journal entry, he wrote that he hallucinated that he was a turd inside a bowel. He was being pushed out, pressure on all sides, and complete with the sensation of smell and taste. The clarity of the perception freaked him out. That was why he left class so abruptly after extraction. After he related his experience, he was the only one of us who didn't laugh at Ben's question about whether he was a firm or loose stool.

Ben told us he unsuccessfully attempted to fall asleep then decided to thrash about as a means of creating stimuli. After he felt completely exhausted he called out to be extricated. The unusual feature of Ben's experience is that he hadn't moved at all during his entire time in the tank. Ben's characterization of the episodes was that they were like dreams, turned nightmarish, because there was no waking up, and they had to be endured until he had the wherewithal to call out to be extracted.

I summarized my episode as best as I could remember. But shouting in French was what I was most interested in and thought it warranted further investigation. Everyone else was just amused.

After our short presentations were completed, Dr. Janis asked if we were ready for another "dip" in the tank. Ben seemed eager, Alec unenthusiastic. While I was apprehensive as well, I was also curious about what the next session would bring. Would there be more French or was that simply an aberration. I wanted to learn more.

We went in the same order as last week.

Ben stayed in a little longer, but was just as freaked out this time. Something about cockroaches everywhere.

Alec's submersion approached ten minutes. He said he tried my technique of meditating. It worked for several seconds before he began choking on imaginary smoky, acrid air.

My turn.

I tried meditating again. Had the sensation of flying. Then I was in a cave feeling my way along a slimy floor, centipedes scurrying over my hands, bats fluttering past my ears. This was creeping me out. I tried to bring myself back to being in a tank of warm water. But my perception was that the cave was flooding. I was being tossed against the cave walls, couldn't breathe.

I don't know why, but I prayed. There was a distinct smell of rotten wood that seemed familiar. I tasted black walnuts, but that was not the wood smell. I had a vision from a heavily-wooded limestone ledge and overhang, high above a wide body of water that seemed to flow around both sides of the escarpment. A fleeting panoramic image but rich in detail. Really quite beautiful. I knew this was an important place. A place I needed to return to, but I sensed being abandoned, alone and afraid. Not just afraid, unmitigated terror. Then exhaustion, the smell of wood again, the feeling I was in a coffin. "Help me! Get me out!"

It took what seemed like several minutes before the welcome piercing light and fresh air. My helmet was off.

"Again with the French," Ben said.

"What did I say?"

"Something about a mountain and a river. Then 'help

me!' I couldn't make it out completely because my French isn't that good. It sounded like you were praying 'Our Father ...' in Latin. I think it was the Lord's Prayer. I recognized parts of it, I used to be an altar boy."

"*You* were an altar boy?" Alec asked sarcastically.

"Yeah, in my wild and crazy youth," Ben retorted. "I've settled down since then."

5

Initially, I was somewhere between amused and intrigued by the sudden onset of speaking in French. But over the last several days I began having nightmares and inexplicable visions. Concerned, I described them to Dan, confident that he would help me understand what was going on. We spent so much time at his apartment off campus that we had time to talk about class informally. Each time I had a nightmare or vision, I related it to Dan, assuming he'd be eager to discuss and investigate this psychological phenomenon. After all, it did commence during his class and was happening to his girlfriend.

But Dan showed little interest and was losing patience with my constant questions about it. His only explanation was xenoglossy or aphasia.

"Aphasia is *loss* of speech, isn't it?" I asked.

"Typically, yes, but the impact on speech varies from individual to individual. The sensory deprivation may have had a temporary effect on your speech center. It isn't uncommon for patients to suffer temporary speech loss from a stroke, coma, or accident and compensate for the loss in some way. You may simply have lost the ability to speak English and compensated with French."

"But I have never spoken French, don't know any French-speaking people, where the hell did the French come from?"

"It had to come from somewhere, Willa. You are probably simply repressing memories or experiences. There is a logical explanation, we just don't know what that explanation is yet."

"Dan, these are not 'repressed memories.' There is no way on God's green earth that I learned to speak fluent French and oh, must have just forgot about it."

"Well, that leaves xenoglossy and that isn't science. Only quacks write about unverifiable fantastic cases of sudden inexplicable ability to speak in a language completely foreign to the subject."

"Oh, you mean just like what has been happening to me?"

"They're just trying to sell some books. That isn't credible evidence."

"You're telling me you don't believe what you personally witnessed, Dan? You think there could be no way that xenoglossy ever occurs, under any circumstance?"

"No, I don't believe that it is a phenomenon. The published cases haven't been verified or were repudiated as fabrications, hoaxes, or diagnostic negligence."

"You believe what you read, but not what you see, is that it? I hoped I could count on you to help me get to the bottom of this."

"If you're asking me to investigate or formally research this, the answer is no. I am not putting my reputation behind some foolishness, just because we haven't found an explanation."

"Well, I'm not giving up on this 'foolishness'! Can you at least suggest a source on xenoglossy?"

"Try Charles Richet, but Willa, don't jeopardize your Ph.D. with an obsessive distraction chasing some memory aberration. This may also be something else altogether. For example, you may be experiencing an acute psychotic episode triggered either by the sensory deprivation or some other recent event. But it wouldn't be appropriate for me to provide professional services, and frankly I'm not comfortable referring you to a colleague."

"I'll keep that in mind," I said, but felt bad immediately because it probably came off as a little bitchy.

But the visions, thoughts, and nightmares were occurring frequently and not just when I was in the tank. I was becoming increasingly concerned and was surprised and disappointed by Dan's lack of support. If he doesn't accept xenoglossy as a possibility, I understand that. But not making an effort to help I don't understand. If he thinks it's an acute psychotic episode, that could be serious and should be right up Dan's alley. This may not be important to the field of psychology, but it was important to me. His dismissal of the whole thing was demeaning.

Just over a year earlier, in December 1969, I applied for the Ph.D. program. Dan was on the faculty review committee for candidates. I was tasked with defending Freud's theories on personality and psychoanalysis. Freud's influence on the field had diminished to the point of being anecdotal. The field was being dominated by contemporary theorists like Harlow, Bandura, and Skinner. Operant conditioning and behavior modification were of particular interest here at the university since the construction of the new primate lab, which was funded specifically for research in behavioral psychology. It was very much in vogue to trash Freud. I had to argue his defense and struggled to find a hypothesis. I finally landed on an approach I thought was logical and had not been aggressively addressed in the literature. My position was that Freud should not be discredited for the analysis, diagnosis, and subsequent treatment of his patients, but only for his assumption that his findings were universally applicable. My primary point was that his patients were so uniquely similar, and specific in time and place that there is no way to duplicate his process. Therefore there was no way to determine, using scientific methodology, the merit of his conclusions. The overwhelming majority of his patients were middle-aged, paranoid, Catholic, Victorian, Austrian women at the turn of the twentieth century. Who is to say his assessment of those ladies wasn't spot-on. His shortcoming instead was concluding that his theory, developed while working with these patients, applied across the board. This is a sampling problem and not uncommon at the time. Use of a hypothesis, control groups, and the scientific method was still evolving during Freud's early career. He should be no more impugned than any other scientist during that era. And the guy stood his ground when his contemporaries laughed at his theories and publicly belittled him. He demonstrated a strength of character and conviction, I would argue. Unfortunately, as I prepared for my presentation, I had little confidence, and frankly thought my defense of Freud was simplistic and largely pointed out the obvious.

I was certain the committee would agree and deny my application to grad school. Later, I was astonished to learn that Dan was impressed with my interpretation. It really wasn't that good. Why would someone as smart as him find my reasoning "powerful" enough to lobby the rest of the review committee to accept me into the program? It didn't seem likely that he would try to ingratiate me, and there was no reason to do me a favor. I guess he just liked it. A month later by coincidence I ended up in his graduate class. He told me over our first coffee date that he dismissed Freud, like many of his colleagues, as "a cigar-chewing, sexually-frustrated Victorian, who saw penises in telephone poles." My argument made him "*slightly*" more sympathetic.

I had been able to make him slightly more sympathetic to Freud then, but evidently not to me and my bizarre experience in the tank.

6

I arrived at the lab early and found Dan already there.

"Dan, I found a couple of very interesting xenoglossy cases, one of them published recently. In each case the subject either began speaking a different language, had memories of a place or time they never experienced, or both. How many documented cases does it take for a pseudo-science to become credible?"

"More than you're going to find. Willa, these are not scientists writing about controlled experiments or verifiable therapy sessions. These are reports of what a few crackpots claim happened to them."

"Well, I'm one of those crackpots, and it's real, whether you think so or not. What I actually experienced is credible enough for me."

"You know that's not what I meant."

"I'm not so sure, because that is precisely what you said."

"What are you guys talking about? I could hear you down the hall," Ben said, as he walked into the lab.

"Xenoglossy. Doctor Janis thinks it's foolishness. I think it describes what has happened to me perfectly."

"Never heard of xenoglossy. What is it?" Ben asked.

After I defined the term and cited a few of the cases, Ben said, "Bummer. That sure sounds like your situation to me."

Defensively Dan said, "You are selectively applying your symptoms to the term. We all do it. We read about the symptoms of a syndrome or disease and suddenly we think we have it because we exhibit some of the characteristics. That is not a diagnosis."

Alec arrived, so Dan said, "Okay, enough about this, it's time for lab."

We each reported on our last deprivation episode and prepared the equipment and safety protocols for this session.

Water temperature was right, the air pump and microphone were tested, and we were ready to begin. We were all getting increasingly comfortable with the experiment. Even Alec was able to joke about his experiences, referring to his first episode as an example of anal retention or latent homosexuality that even Freud would have been proud of.

While Ben and Alec took their turns, I thought about the increasing frequency and intensity of strange, seemingly unrelated images and sensations I had been having. Not just speaking French, but sights, smells, tastes, and those powerful feelings of being trapped, abandoned, lost, and the sudden onset of sheer terror. It was like doing a dream interpretation on visions and memories I was having both awake and asleep. Inexact, but possibly revealing insight into something repressed.

My turn.

My preferred approach continued to be the use of my meditation regimen, but instead of suggesting tingling on the top of my head, which didn't work out well my last session, I focused on the inevitable flashes of dancing light I perceived in the total darkness. The lights seemed to become stars. I thought that would be a good benign focal point to keep my stress in check. I felt as though I were on my back looking up at the night sky—the sky you only see when you're away from the city. The night sky bisected by the Milky Way with each constellation clearly visible. The light transitioned into a fire, a campfire, and a series of sensations—sitting on hard, cold ground, a taste of peppers, and tending plants on a farm. Then I felt like I was running through the darkness, held up by branches and thorns pulling at my clothes. Then quiet, and a vision of a river. I was swimming against the current, then walking through heavy brush, each footstep sinking deep into mud. I was struggling toward a towering, wooded island with a steep escarpment. A beautiful young girl and a Star of David, a bull charging at me like I was a matador ... "Get me out!"

By my next session in the tank a week later, I felt I was persevering better and had been able to delay the onset of hallucinations, but only delay them. Before I screamed out, in French of course, I was certain that I was buried alive. In the blackness, I could taste and smell the damp wood of what I assumed was my coffin pressing on my sides and back.

I was in full panic attack mode when the welcoming light shone through my helmet. Alec and Ben were attending me after pulling me out of the tank. It took a moment for me to regain my bearings and recognize that this was reality, and that the disturbing perception of being buried alive was just a delusion.

Each subsequent session grew in intensity. The hallucinations were vivid and clear. Without external stimulus, I wasn't able to discern that the frightening sensations I was experiencing in the tank were just dreams, until I was out of the tank and back to reality. While Ben, Alec, and I knew that our experiences were triggered by the sensory deprivation, we had each gone through several episodes and learned in class that the results were typical for the experiment, but it didn't help mitigate the sheer terror we often experienced while in the tank.

My experiences were similar to the others in many ways. However, my "tank" hallucinations and perceptions included the sudden onset of speaking French and, based on the visions and other clues, channeling the experiences of what I interpreted was from some French guy a couple hundred years ago. The delusions continued to recur in the tank, but also in my dreams and as daytime visions and thoughts, without abatement. Ben and Alec described their hallucinations as wide ranging, random, and *occurring only when they were in the tank.*

I tried to conceal my fear about what was happening to me, but was growing increasingly troubled.

7

It was the weekend Dan was meeting my parents. I drove to my parent's house a couple hours before Dan. It had snowed four inches the night before, but for early March in Wisconsin, the roads were in good driving condition. I'd been looking forward to this and couldn't wait to introduce him. Dan is special in a lot of ways, and he is the first boyfriend I'm bringing home to "meet the parents." Dan planned to return to Madison after dinner. Mom was disappointed. She made my brother Mike's old bedroom into a guest room and was hoping to use it for that purpose at some point. I would stay at home for the weekend.

When Dan arrived, the four of us sat in the living room making small talk and getting my parents and Dan acquainted. After a short time, I left with Mom to help her get dinner ready, leaving Dan alone with my dad. They were talking intently when I returned.

"Uh oh, this looks like trouble. What are you two talking about?" I said.

"Politics," Dad said.

"Isn't that one of the topics you're supposed to *avoid* in social settings?"

"More about Vietnam than politics," Dan clarified.

"Unless you guys plan to call the Pentagon to alert them to your findings, it's time for dinner," I said.

"I'm too hungry to call. Let's eat," Dad said.

Trying to avoid any awkward silences, Mom took over

the conversation. I know she was just being a mom and trying to engage Dan, but her ceaseless questions didn't give the poor guy a chance to eat his dinner. I could tell she really liked Dan. In fact, if she were thirty years younger and single, I think she would have married him on the spot.

Dad was a tougher read. But his body language and forced smiles suggested that he was not as impressed with Dan as I thought he would be.

Dan turned down an after-dinner drink and stayed for another hour. During a brief lapse in the conversation he stood up, thanked Mom for a great dinner and Dad for the drink offer, said he had a long drive back to Madison, and despite the hospitality, he would have to leave. Mom hugged him, Dad shook his hand, and I kissed him, a "job well done" kiss.

After helping Mom clean up I joined Dad on the porch. He was sipping brandy.

"So, what do think of Dan?" Evidently, my dad decided not to give me his unvarnished assessment of Dan. All he told me was "the boy seems nice."

"The boy!" I said. "He is thirty-one, has a Ph.D. in psychology from Madison and is a respected professor."

"I didn't mean to be disrespectful, Willa. It was just a poor word choice. He's very successful in his field, has a great job, what's not to like?"

Dad thinks he's being coy. I can tell he's not impressed just by reading his eyes. But I can't tell what it is.

"I'm not letting you get away with that banality."

"Banality? Willa, I'm just an old logger."

"Okay Dad, in 'old logger' technical jargon, cut the bullshit. Tell me what you really think. Even if I wasn't a pre-doctorial psychology student, I am your daughter, and you haven't been able to fool me for years."

"Oh, now she tells me."

"So what do you *really* think of Dan?"

"What do you mean? I told you I thought he was nice. He does seem like a nice enough guy. He's doing very well for himself. Good career. As long as he treats you well, respects and appreciates you, I am fine with him."

"Fine with him! Wow, that is some kind of endorsement. Come on Dad, cut the crap. What is your impression of him?"

"You're relentless, you know that, Willa? Okay. For what it's worth, I think he is very talented in some ways but nothing to write home about in other ways. Academically he excels, but he just didn't impress me as a man who thinks for himself."

"What do you mean, doesn't think for himself?"

"Look, honey, I'm not comfortable giving a first impression on that. I talked to the guy for maybe one and a half hours."

"You're the one who said he can't think for himself. What makes you say that?"

"My last comment on this is, that no matter what the topic was, if you strip away the quotes and reciting what he's read, there just wasn't much there. That's all."

"Well, some really smart people at the university have a very different opinion of him than yours."

"What about you, Willa?"

"Yes. I think he is very smart, too."

"Well, your opinion is really the only one that counts, honey. Not some old logger."

"I wouldn't have asked if I didn't want to hear from that old logger. But of all the things that you could have said, 'not thinking for himself' was the last one I expected. Dan is brilliant."

"You know him a lot better than I do."

My mom walked in. "Oh, hi honey. It's so nice having you here. It just doesn't seem like home unless you or your brothers are here. What have you and your dad been talking about?"

"Dan."

"What a nice young man. He was so polite, and you didn't tell me he was so handsome."

"Dad didn't like him and thinks he's a twit."

27

"Will Heinlein! How could you say that?" Mom asked.

"Oh, for Christ's sake. Willa, you know that's not what I said. I am having another drink. Either of you want something?"

I'll have another chat with Dad later and press him for details. I just can't imagine what Dan could've said that led my dad to be so down on him. And if Dad said what he said after first meeting Dan, that probably means he feels even more strongly than he is letting on. He doesn't want to hurt my feelings. I'm surprised and disappointed by Dad's assessment.

8

I got up the next morning at seven. Dad was already up and on the sun porch with his coffee and newspaper. Mom was still asleep. I poured myself a cup from his pot and joined him.

"Good morning, honey! Did you sleep okay?"

"Good morning, Dad. Yeah, pretty well. But I kept thinking about what you said last night."

"You mean about Dan. Look Willa, I'm sorry I said what I said. I have no right to judge that young man and no business sharing my half-baked opinions. I wish I had kept my mouth shut. I'm not the one dating him."

I think Dad was afraid he might come across like his Uncle Friedrich did when his cousin Anna first introduced Michael. That was just after Dad got here from Germany. Friedrich was a bigoted old man who nearly ruined his relationship with his daughter. If I was Anna, I don't think I could ever forgive him for his anti-Polish diatribes to my fiancé. Uncle Michael seemed to have moved past it, but I'll bet he never forgot. I guess Dad didn't want that to happen to us. Oh, I know he embarrasses the hell out of me sometimes and he will never quite catch up with the times, but bless his heart, he's trying to avoid creating a fuss unnecessarily. And, you know, over time I've learned to appreciate the fact that he has a remarkable ability to read people. I'd be foolish not to hear him out.

"Well that cat is out of the bag now, Dad, and I'm curious

what he could have said that prompted you to form that 'half-baked' opinion. It's important to me. Don't candy-coat it, I can take it."

"Oh shit. Okay. In the past three or four years we've had the assassinations of Martin Luther King and Bobby Kennedy, race riots, whole sections of cities burning down, and that quagmire in Vietnam. I was looking forward to hearing what a psychology professor's take on all this was. He didn't have much to say. So okay, I thought I could at least learn about what the hell was happening on campus. Every time I turn on the news, there's rioting, looting, tear gas. It scares the hell out of me with you there. Dan seemed like the perfect source. A psychology professor, smart guy and he's right there. I was interested in hearing his objective, informed take on all that. But when I asked Dan to tell me what he thought about the rioting on campus and should we be sending kids to fight in Vietnam? And why violence was the way college kids chose to protest? All I got were recited newspaper articles and something from *Time Magazine*. Dan answered with the number of US fatalities, the cost of the war, and cities where rioting occurred last week, last month, and year-to-date. No, professor, I asked you what the hell *you* think about this shit. Blank stare. Evidently, he doesn't know what he thinks. Nope. He can quote the hell out of any articles related to the question, but he can't seem to go beyond that. Some moron blew up a chemistry lab in Madison seven months ago, 3:42 a.m., August 24, 1970 according to the professor. Killed some poor guy working late trying to finish a project. Why? What's going on? No thoughts from the professor. That crap 'bring the war home,' and all the rioting, that's what worries the hell out of me. I wasn't testing him, but wanted to understand what was happening in Madison. Look what happened to you, May of last year. Tear-gassed and clubbed by a cop, and you just stepped out of the bookstore on State Street. Isn't that right? I don't think you ever told Mom and me that whole story. Since you're making me come clean, I think it's only fair play if you tell me the full story about what happened to you."

"I didn't want to worry you unnecessarily. There isn't a lot more to it than I told you before. While I was checking out my books for summer school, I saw hundreds of kids running down State Street toward campus. When I stepped out onto the sidewalk in front of the bookstore, a tear gas canister landed at my feet. I couldn't believe how quickly it worked. Within a second or two I couldn't breathe or see anything, and the searing pain in my eyes and lungs was incredible. That's when one of the cops in riot gear hit me with his baton. I fell down and laid in the street coughing and gasping until the line of cops moved past and the tear gas cleared. Ben, from my grad class, stumbled upon me and got a friend he was with to help get me to the medical clinic. Ben thought I had been rioting too and told me I was one of the 'ballsy' ones that rushed the cops. I had no idea what he was talking about, but appreciated the help. I tried to tell them I was just in the wrong place at the wrong time, but I'm not sure I was completely coherent yet. Anyway, I was fine. The nurse at the clinic flushed my eyes with a saline solution, gave me some oxygen, put gauze on the head wound, and told me I might want to sit the next riot out. I started to explain that I just walked out of a store, but she was on to the next kid. There must have been twenty of us in there. Anyway, that's really all there was to it."

"All there was to it! Geez Willa, if I had known all that back then, I would have driven down there and pulled you out of school right then and there. What did Dan say about it?"

"He was sympathetic but said I should have been more careful. That I must have done something to provoke the police, or make them think I was a rioter. He said the 'police don't just club people.'"

"But isn't that exactly what they did?"

"Yeah, it is. I mean I literally just stepped onto the sidewalk. I don't know what I could have done differently. But Dan thinks I must have done something."

"I used to think that all the rioting and burning was just crazy radicals on campus. But the police aren't helping matters when they pull this shit. Look at Kent State. The National Guard opened fire on those kids. Killed four. Hell, one of them was like you, just walking to class. They claimed they felt 'threatened' by the crowd of students and fired to quell the threat. You know how close the nearest student was to them when they shot? Over two hundred feet away. How much of a threat are unarmed students at that distance? Your brother Mike was in Vietnam for over a year. He'd never shoot or whack some kid on the head. Hell, I was in the army, too. It was a long time ago but as far as I'm concerned, if fifty National Guardsmen in riot gear with live ammo felt threatened by a bunch of kids halfway across campus, they're not fit for duty. When I asked Dan about that, he told me the same thing he told you—the students must have been attacking the guards because that's what the report said. That just sounds inane to me. I know we only talked for an hour or so, but he never once answered a question directly. Just quoted something. Hell, I can read. I was just disappointed that's all. I hoped I would get some insights that I don't have and can't get being up here."

"Wow, I asked for it. So, he's not up on his current events? Is that it?"

"No, that is *not* it. He knows his current events, to the minute. He just doesn't have ... an opinion, doesn't have a thought on how to resolve this stuff, doesn't even see any correlation between the war, draft, rioting, drugs, the damn music you listen to. It scares me with you in the middle of all that, especially considering what happened to you. I want to understand what's going on. Like I said, I wasn't testing him. I just wanted to get his take on things. I just don't know what's going on and was disappointed that I didn't learn anything, that's all."

"Dad, I asked and you told me. That was hard, probably on both of us. But I appreciate your honesty. Maybe his perspective on something else won't disappoint you."

"Good morning, you two! Any coffee left?"

"Good morning, Mom. Yeah, I think there's still a cup or so in the pot."

9

I called Dan that night. I wanted to be sure he got back safely, and to get his view of my parents. He admitted that he was a little nervous, my mom's cooking was "superb," and my dad knows a lot about logging and reads the news. When I pressed him a little on my dad, Dan added, "But, for someone who's up on the news, your dad didn't even know when the physics lab was blown up."

That wasn't like Dan. He's rarely defensive or condescending toward anyone. No, he just retrieves one more citation out of his endless memory trove until the other person concedes the point. There was something else. I assume it's my dad's doggedness. He can be a real pain in the ass when he gets his mind set on something.

It was clear, though, that they didn't exactly hit it off. For the most part I understand Dan's view, but I'm struggling with my dad's. If things progress the way I think they're going, then they could be spending a lot more time together. These are the two most important men in my life. While I don't expect them to be best buddies, it would be nice if they respected each other and at least got along.

10

That night I had another nightmare of vivid coherent visions. My arms were full carrying something through the woods. I crested a steep hill and watched as six or seven Indians butchered three men on the bank of a river. The Indians fanned out and I felt terrified that they were looking for me. I dropped what I was carrying, slowly backed down from the crest of the hill, turned and ran through the forest. Branches, briars, hidden pitfalls slowed my desperate attempt to escape. I found a canoe on the bank of a wide river, but left it there and kept walking. I started down-stream, but reversed course. Ahead of me in the distance was an island in the river, rising straight up. At that point I woke up, sweating and exhausted.

My mother came into my room and asked if I was all right. She heard me shout something and wondered if I was having a bad dream. I tried to make light of it and said I had just been restless.

The next morning I was up early, made my coffee, and wrote down all of the visions, voices, sounds, and smells I could remember having during my submersions and now in nightmares.

Everything spoken was in French. I was on either a river or long narrow lake, but I remember a strong current I was paddling against. The Indians carried muskets and hatchets. The black walnuts, the rocky escarpment on an island rising high out of the water. The smell of wood, the feeling of confinement, fear, praying, desperate for help. It seemed that the island I saw in the dream last night could have been the same one I envisioned two weeks earlier in the tank, only the perspective was different. Last night I was on the water looking at the island, but my previous vision was from a ledge on a cliff on the island looking out over the water. There was more but I needed to put my session notes from class together with my dreams. This dream was different. Not only in content but here it is six hours later and instead of evaporating into a fleeting memory as my dreams typically did, this one remained, with total recall and absolute clarity.

I packed up, waited till my parents got up so I could say goodbye, then left for Madison.

11

I was looking forward to the next deprivation session. Not because I enjoyed them, but because of the mystery of all this. It was clear I was channeling someone's thoughts and feelings. While it started with the first submersion, the dreams, visions, sensations, and specific thoughts now occur regularly day and night. My nighttime dreams aren't the usual disjointed array of random thoughts or images, but more an infusion of memory of experiences I never had.

Weird. Last night I had another dream. It was like being submerged because it was dark and without any sounds, but I was cold, terrified, and seemingly confined in a narrow, tight space. It was like I was buried alive. This was starting to frighten me. Dreams and visions become delusions when you believe them despite overwhelming evidence to the contrary and your normal daily behavior is being affected. Other than the increase in anxiety I don't think my normal behavior has changed, yet.

I included a description of the dreams during my weekly presentation summarizing the previous week's deprivation experience. Dan, Ben, and Alec looked at me like I was crazy. Ben summed up their look by making an attempt at an eerie "oooooh" sound, then said "far out."

"Okay, okay," I said, "let's get started."

Dan told us about our mid-term test a week from tomorrow and the fifteen-page paper summarizing our research to date, due at the same time. Ben and Alec groaned at the timing.

Dan ignored their editorial and took us through the obligatory submersion safety checklist before we began.

We went in the same order as before. Our submersion times had been increasing as we adapted to the reduced sensory environment.

It didn't take long into my session for the visions and memories to begin. A beautiful young girl with huge hair or wearing a wig, I knew her. And writing. Frantic writing using what looked like a stubby pencil or pen like I used in art class in the sixth grade. I was writing by dim light—a candle or campfire. Page after page I wrote in precise cursive. Despite seeing myself writing the words, I wasn't able to make out most of what I wrote except for a few words, like *les renards*, Father Charles, and Jean LeFay. Even though I didn't know what I was writing, somehow I was aware that it was important. Suddenly I felt like I was buried alive. Wood walls closing in, stale air that smelled of rotting wood, of death. "Get me out!"

Dan put on his professional face in class and said all the right things. Encouraging me to record each perception and note any links, repetitions, or new phenomenon in my summary.

Privately he was clearly losing patience with my obsessing on what I was experiencing.

Over dinner at his apartment that night I spoke excitedly about the young woman, the writing, and the feeling of being buried alive. I talked through the common themes— French, wilderness, Indians, eighteenth-century woman based on the fashion, *les renards*, which I learned meant *fox* in French, canoes, and the sensation of being buried alive. I concluded that I was channeling a French explorer.

Dan had had enough. "You are talking like a psychotic. These are delusions and hallucinations you're having. You don't really believe that you're 'channeling' some French guy from the two hundred years ago, do you?"

"Yes, I do. Because the only other possible explanation is that I suddenly developed a psychosis. While that conclusion may appeal to you, I much prefer the former. What is happening is not unprecedented in literature, and objectively, that diagnosis seems as appropriate as yours."

"What diagnosis? Xenoglossy? Channeling? Reincarnation? You're not diagnosing, you're trying to rationalize delusions. That's what psychosis is."

"Bullshit, Dan! Psychosis is the belief and profound alteration to normal conduct, despite overwhelming evidence to the contrary. It sure doesn't seem overwhelming to me. Or to Ben and Alec or to the doctors documenting cases similar to mine. You don't have an explanation either. Do you?"

"Delusions and hallucinations are my diagnosis. And that diagnosis seems pretty irrefutable."

"So I'm a crazy broad?"

"Not crazy, delusional."

"Well, I'm going to find out one way or another."

"How do you think you're going to 'find out'?"

"I'm going to find out who the hell this guy is. There is enough evidence for me to start researching and I get more evidence every damn night."

"You're confusing dreams with evidence, Willa. You sound anxious, depressed, and obsessive. These are symptoms that can interfere with normal behavior and when they are paired with delusions, are pathological."

"I know that. But as long as I am functioning normally, then I am going to pursue the cause of the sudden onset of these nightmares and sensations. At this point that's all I have to go on now isn't it, *Doctor Janis?*"

"You have a mid-term and paper due in less than a week. You don't have time to go off on some wild goose chase."

"That 'wild goose chase' is going to be my paper. This is what is happening to me as a direct and irrefutable result of our sensory deprivation project. It is what I have experienced. It is what I have documented. It is my paper!"

"Willa, I don't know what to say."

41

"How about, 'how can I help you?' Or, 'if I were you here's where I'd start?'"

"I can't in good conscious encourage you to do this."

"Well, I'm going to research this. From both psychology literature and the historical record."

"Okay, okay. I have looked through the psych material already and as far as I'm concerned there isn't anything there. But I can justify bolstering up my French-Canadian history. I will help you with that."

"I appreciate it. I just wish ... never mind."

"Just wish what?"

"Nothing. I'm just glad you're going to help. I've been thinking about the visions I've had and it seems the logical place to begin is to try to find the island. It would probably be something frequented by French travelers during that period."

"You've reported a variety of perceptions. Why look for the island?"

"First, it seems to be the most frequently recurring vision. It must have some significance. Second, the visions are so clear, I think if I actually see the site, I will be able to recognize it."

"Even after deforestation, erosion, roads, and houses?"

"Yes, I think so."

"So where do you want to start?"

"Let's start at the library and then go to the historical society."

After class the next day we walked to the library. Dan left me in the history section while he went to do some research on, of all things, electro-convulsive shock. What about brushing up on his French-Canadian history? I pulled half a dozen texts on European history and French exploration and settlements in the Great Lakes area. Two nights ago, I had a particularly disturbing dream and I thought this would be an opportunity to see if there was any historical credence to it.

In the first part of my dream, I was marching in military

formation toward an enemy line that was moving quickly toward us. I looked down my line and saw what looked like an entire army. The troops were clad in light gray coats, tricorner felt hats, and carried muskets. We stopped and were ordered in French to present arms. I saw a cloud of smoke rise from the enemy position, and within a second I heard the distinct thuds of lead balls striking those around me, followed by the delayed distant report of the muskets fired at us. The soldier to my left fell dead with a gaping wound in his neck. The order to take aim was barely discernable above the din followed immediately by "FIRE!" which I did. Mechanically, I started to reload. Just as I raised my musket to fire, a second volley hit our ranks.

I stood steady and fired when the order was given. We were ordered to right face. A second line of enemy troops was descending a hill on our flank led by a cavalry brigade that had sabers drawn and were advancing quickly. I recognized the Union Jack on the enemy's flag and knew they were English. Our lines to my right broke. My line did not. We reloaded and fired at the advancing cavalry. As the cavalry sliced into our disorganized right flank we were ordered to retreat toward a bridge. Our troops were routed and bottlenecked trying to cross a pontoon bridge. Our lieutenant ordered us to reform and reload. With the cavalry nearly upon us, we fired. At such close range our volley was deadly accurate and the charge turned and circled wide to reform. Again we retreated and reformed, this time at the bridge, loading, aiming, and firing another volley at the advancing enemy. By then the bridge was largely clear of our troops and we began to cross. I was struck in the side and fell. I felt searing pain, then only warm liquid running down my leg. That's when I woke up. Like other dreams that started after the first submersion, this one was vivid, incredibly real, and etched into my memory. I remember every detail.

Based on the muskets and uniforms and dates the French and English were at war, I started my research in the time frame of 1650–1750. While I didn't expect to solve anything today, maybe I would add a piece to the puzzle.

So, we have a portrait of Louis XIV, king of France from 1643 to 1715. Nice hair. Oh, it looks like he was quite the ladies' man. Let's see...two wives; four, no, five known mistresses. Expanding Versailles into a spectacular palace took place during his reign. Now, which war might have been in the dream?

You're kidding me. The Thirty Years War, War of Devolution, Franco-Dutch, Scanian War, War of Reunions, War of Spanish Succession, King William's War, Queen Anne's War— all between 1600 and 1700. Is that all these guys did?

Okay, sleuth, let's sleuth. Had to be France against England since I saw the Union Jack in the attack. That rules out the Thirty Years War. That was mostly Germans, Swedes, Spanish, and Bosnians. Also rules out the Franco-Dutch because France and England were on the same side. Rule out Scanian and War of Reunions because England wasn't involved. King William and Queen Anne Wars were fought primarily in North America and involved allied Indian tribes on both sides. I didn't see any Indians during the battle.

Okay, that leaves the War of Devolution and Spanish Succession. What was different about them? What do I remember from the dream? Firing the musket several times. Let's check out firearms in the French army in 1650. Here's a picture of a Piker and Mousquetaire of that era. I didn't see any Pikers in the dream, and what's that thing the other guy is holding? It looks like a musket with a rope dangling from the middle. Says here it's called a matchlock or arquebus. That doesn't look anything like I remember. Next picture shows a circa 1700 French soldier, a Fusilier, with a musket and his light gray uniform looks more like what I remember. So I guess it must have been the Spanish War of Succession.

What was that war all about? It seems King Louis wanted his grandson, Philip, to take the Spanish throne after Charles II died without an heir and willed the throne to Philip. England, Holland, Prussia, and Austria didn't like the idea. Too much power for France and Catholics. As much as I hate this stuff, I'm actually getting into it. I feel like a detective. So the most recent dream was about that war, but I also have visions and memories of forests, Indians, canoes, and stockades. Maybe those are of King William's or Queen Anne's wars? Either this guy was a career soldier and fought in two wars on two continents, or I'm channeling two different guys. Maybe there will be more information at the historical society. Ordinarily I wouldn't have spent a minute reading about what happened a couple hundred years ago if I didn't have to. But I have to, even though what I'm learning isn't providing much help. At least I know the approximate time frame. I've got to keep digging and try to figure out why I am going crazy ... or, or I'll go crazy!

Oh, here comes Dan.

"All done?" he asked.

"Yeah, let's go to the historical society and see what they have."

We chatted about what we learned during our separate research while we walked the few blocks down State Street to the historical society. The archives were deep in the bowels of the building. Except for a heavy wooden table and four chairs, the cavernous room was completely occupied by row after row of metal shelving piled with labeled cardboard boxes. The archivist emerged from behind us and asked what we were interested in seeing. I told her we would like to see any maps, memoirs, or first-hand accounts of late seventeenth- or early eighteenth-century French exploration of the Great Lakes. I sat and prepared for an extensive wait while the archivist searched.

Dan and I were astonished when she emerged within a minute toting one cardboard box and an acid-free folder. The content consisted of reprints of paintings depicting the historical events—fur trade and Great Lakes native people—and third person descriptions of Father Louis Joliet's and Jacques Marquette's travels and missionary work. The folder held a half-dozen eighteenth-century maps, which proved the most useful to our purpose. After donning white gloves, Dan and I carefully inspected the maps, looking for any demarcations that could be the site in my visions.

The most relevant map was dated 1718 and included Wisconsin, northern Michigan and bordering Great Lakes. I don't know why but the name of the mapmaker, L'Isle, was familiar, important, and clearly related to my visions. It was like a mnemonic device. Once I saw the name, it triggered a series of recollections about the man, even what he looked like. I didn't tell Dan this. He finally seemed willing to help out and I didn't want to spook him before we even got started.

The 1718 map consisted primarily of the main waterways, rivers, portages, the word *Les Renards* written across a wide section of the map, and a few familiar-looking sites and names—Baye Verti and islands at the north end of the bay, Prairie du Chien, and Mackinac Island.

"Maybe Mackinac Island is the place to start. It has high bluffs, was a historic French-Canadian post, and a stopover point for French explorers traveling into Wisconsin. We could stop in Door County on the way up and look at Washington Island, too, it's drawn but unnamed on the map at the end of Door Peninsula. If you come, we can make a long weekend of it," I said.

Dan agreed to join me as long as he could fit it in. I probably talked Dan into it, but he was finally attempting to be considerate. We decided traveling over spring break would be ideal. I was excited to explore the two areas we were going to visit. The images I had of the island in my dreams and in the tank are so clear, I am confident it won't take much exploring to determine which one it is.

On Thursday night we drove from Madison to the tip of Door County. We spent the night at a little motel. I was surprised that it was so expensive to stay there, considering that it was early April and still the off-season for tourists who come in droves to the area in the summer and fall. Early Friday morning we took a ferry to Washington Island.

Beautiful place, but nothing there looked familiar and none of the place names like L'Isle des Poux, Huron Island, Potawatomi Island, triggered a memory or feeling. This area wasn't it. We left for Mackinac Island early in the afternoon. It was a long drive. We ran out of things to talk about the last four hours. I swear we nearly hit deer crossing the highway five different times over the last 150 miles.

We checked into the Grand Hotel on Mackinac Island Friday night and explored the island on bicycles all day Saturday. It was colder than Door County and residual snow, mostly piles from shoveling off the sidewalks, was still around. On Sunday morning we spent some time with the curator of a small museum not far from the hotel. Dan started reading from a book, *History of Mackinac Island.*

"It says here that the French colonized from the Great Lakes all the way down the Mississippi River," Dan read aloud. "There have got to be a thousand islands that could be what you're looking for."

"That's wrong," I said.

"What's wrong? That there aren't a thousand islands in all that territory?"

"No. That the French colonized the whole area. There were a few small farming communities around their forts, but the French didn't colonize much beyond Montreal and Quebec. They were missionaries, soldiers, and traders, not settlers. Colonizing would have just pissed off their Indian allies," I said.

"What are you talking about? It says right here in this *history* book that they colonized."

"You saw the 1718 map by L'Isle in Madison. There weren't town names or evidence of colonies. Besides, *Un roi, une loi, une foi*—one king, one law, one faith—that doctrine prohibited entrepreneurs, farmers, or religious sects from immigrating to New France to colonize. The French wanted to trade with the Indians and the Jesuits wanted to convert the Indians to Christianity. Colonizing would have antagonized them and made it difficult to do either," I said.

"How do you know that?" Dan asked incredulously.

"I don't know. I just know."

"Well, it says here they colonized, and I tend to believe history books when it comes to history."

"You believe what you choose. I know what I know. Think about it Dan, can you name a city other than New Orleans, Quebec, and Montreal that the French fully colonized? No. Green Bay, Saint Louis, and the other French sites were missions, forts, and trading posts. The people only came later, much later. How many French settlements were in the Louisiana Purchase? Parts of ten states and a hundred years later, there still weren't French settlements in ninety-nine percent of it. They were here to convert some Catholics, trade for furs, and outflank the English through alliances with the Indians."

"Willa, it says right here in front of me that the French colonized. They're not making this up."

"Like I said Dan, I know what I know."

Well, it turns out that Mackinac was not *the* island, but I would love to go back when I had some time. What a beautiful place. No cars, just bikes and horse-drawn wagons. Yes, I would come back, just not with Dan. He couldn't leave quick enough and complained about it on and off all the way back to Madison. Nothing to do there, too long a drive, roads aren't marked correctly, deer darting into the road every few miles, and on and on. I was disappointed, too, but only because that was my best guess and that wasn't the place.

He made it clear that he didn't intend to do research with me again, or even consider going on my next planned trip that I told him I'd like to take to the Apostle Islands in Lake Superior. "It's not a vacation if we have to drive thirteen hours of the weekend," he whined. Fine. I planned the next one alone.

Once we were back, I called my brother Mike and asked him if he'd like to go to Bayfield with me in the next week or two. I said I was interested in doing research, but kept it vague. He agreed to come along and said he was actually excited to have a reason to drive up to Lake Superior. He had been talking with Dad and Uncle Michael about finding out if there were any old-growth hardwood logs sunk in the harbors of Lake Superior. If there were, they could figure out if they were preserved and economically retrievable. If so, they might set up a small operation there to pull them out, dry the logs, and mill the lumber.

Mike is four years older than me and two years older than my other brother, Peter. Mike is married to Joanie and has a toddler, Annie. He got back from Vietnam almost three years ago. He got into ROTC his freshman year in college and part of the deal was that he'd enlist afterward. Back in 1962, Mike was a freshman, President Kennedy was still alive, and we were only sending "advisors" to Vietnam. My dad warned him that's how most wars start out, but Mike thought it was the right thing for him to do at the time. Sure enough, in 1965 when he graduated, off he went. Thank God he came back okay, but he doesn't like to talk about "Nam" much.

Brother Peter took a big risk. In 1970, the second year of the draft lottery, he let his number ride hoping they wouldn't get all the way up to 201, or whatever number he drew. He lucked out. They didn't draft that high. Close to it, but he was out of the woods.

After getting to Mike's house in Ladysmith for our adventure, I had a chance to talk with Joanie, hold Annie, and visit for a while until Mike got antsy and wanted to get going. He drove. During the drive he explained to me that when the Apostle Islands were logged they could only use barges or float the logs strapped to pontoons from the islands to the mainland. I half listened as he told me about how hardwood logs don't float and they were so damn heavy the barges could only carry a half dozen at a time. That wasn't efficient. So they tried chaining logs together between several barges and sail the flotilla to port. Lake Superior is unpredictable and can get pretty rough without warning. When that happened, the flotilla would break apart and many of the logs would sink. Once in the harbor, loading the huge cumbersome logs was difficult and many fell into the water and sank to the bottom. Those were the logs Mike was interested in learning more about. Dad and Uncle Michael knew some of the loggers involved in harvesting the islands in Lake Superior and they were sure there were hundreds of these huge virgin maple, birch, and ash logs sitting at the bottom of the lake. Find the ones in shallow water and it may be economical to salvage them, if the cold lake water preserved them. He wanted to poke around and see what he could find out. Maybe talk to a few old-timers.

We both had fun reminiscing and making fun of Mom and Dad's idiosyncrasies, their redundant advice, and generally catching up during the drive. With me being away at school and him working and having a family of his own, we only saw each other at holidays. Before that, he was in Vietnam and I didn't see him at all during his enlistment. During the holidays when everyone is together, it is hard to get time with anyone long enough for a meaningful conversation. This drive seemed to go a lot faster and was more enjoyable than going to Mackinac Island with Dan.

When we got to Bayfield, I found the ferry pier and waited for the next run out to the islands while Mike stayed in town to check around. The ice was out and the ferry had just started running again. We planned to meet when we both accomplished our respective objectives at a cafe near the pier, have something to eat, and drive back to Mike's house in Ladysmith.

I was excited with anticipation hoping to see a landscape that looked like the one in my visions. The tour ferry circled and weaved among the chain of islands. I was glad I remembered to bring binoculars. Unfortunately, they didn't help. The guide was knowledgeable, but the excursion turned out to be unproductive. The distinguishing characteristics were wave erosion caves, a unique environment with moose and wolf populations, Ojibwa Indian archeological sites, and the like. While this was all interesting, it wasn't "my" island.

They were all too big and without the steep outcropping I clearly envisioned. While I knew lake islands wouldn't have a river current, I thought water flow between islands, or in the case of Mackinac the narrowing of the lake, could create the same perception. It didn't. This wasn't it either.

We were both finished by two o'clock that afternoon, had a sandwich at the café and left.

Michael asked me how the tour went. I tried to put a positive spin on my disappointment. Instead of telling him it was cold, windy, and I was still feeling queasy from the wave bouncing, I said I really enjoyed seeing the islands even though it was not what I was looking for.

He said a couple of the old-timers Dad knew showed him several spots where they were certain hundreds of huge logs were resting on the bottom of the bay. But they all agreed that getting the logs to the surface and moving them to a drying facility would be daunting. I wondered why it would be so difficult since they obviously were able to haul a lot of those logs out from the harbor sixty years ago. He reminded me that waterlogged wood could weigh up to twice as much as when just cut, making a huge difference.

I was losing hope, and shared some of my visions and why it was important for me to find this specific location with Mike. He seemed more amused than concerned about my compulsion and tried to cheer me up on the way back to Ladysmith. He suggested I check out the Chippewa Flowage and St. Croix River and maybe the Mississippi. We figured each river would have been a well-known water route among early explorers. They each had a myriad of islands and close enough to home that I could drive there and back in a day. The Mississippi seemed too big to tackle without doing a lot of homework, so I thought I'd try the other two rivers first.

If that doesn't work, Mike said I should talk to Dad or Uncle Michael about the location I was looking for. Having been loggers, buying and selling land, and hunting and fishing across the northern third of the state since the

1920s, they knew the area, topography, and waterways as well as anyone.

"I'm afraid they're going to think I'm wacko."

"Is that a clinical term, doctor?"

"At this rate I'm a lot closer to being a patient than I am at becoming a doctor of psychotherapy."

Mike's suggestions were good. I would plan a trip to drive along the St. Croix and Chippewa to see if anything jumped out at me as being significant. And if nothing panned out, why not ask Dad? These are long shots, but so is this whole damn thing.

I spent the night with Mike's family. I couldn't sleep again and laid awake most of the night thinking about my predicament. I was conflicted. Should I continue the search for clues to the origin and meaning of my memories and visions and try piecing together what is happening? Or simply stop going into the tank and admit to myself what Dan has been telling me from the beginning, that my delusions are interfering with my normal behavior, and that I should treat them as an illness, not a puzzle. That choice was troubling because the hallucinations and haunting memories occur all day and every night. Will they just stop on their own? Will therapy help me? Which symptoms do I seek treatment for? The delusions? But I have also developed this manic, obsessive approach to finding out the source and meaning of these memories and visions. This has made me increasingly depressed and sleep-deprived. This is my field of study. I have read all about this stuff, taken the class tests, and seemly know the subject well. But now that it's me and it's real, I don't have any more insights than anyone else. Dan doesn't seem to, either. Although I'm not sure if he doesn't know what to do for me or doesn't want to get in the middle of my problems. Either way, knowing the star professor of the psych department hasn't helped me at all, and frankly has let me down.

I decided that for the time being, as long as I could function with a semblance of normalcy, I would try to persevere.

Maybe the delusions will dissipate if I find out more about the memories, and Dan may be more inclined to be an advocate and actively seek solutions if our relationship strengthens. Unfortunately, we have taken a step or two backward and grown apart. He has become cooler, less engaged, and my symptoms are becoming more evident. It's often hard for me to get anything done. I don't feel like eating, can't concentrate, I just want to curl up in a ball. Then I get motivated again, and energized to renew my investigation of the cause for these persistent nightmares, memories, and visions.

12

Three weeks after the trip with Mike I drove back home on a Friday night hoping I could get some studying done and make a little progress on my next paper. I didn't have to get back for a class until Tuesday afternoon. There were only three classes left, the semester ends next week. Dan gave me a B- on the first paper. The paper was damn good. But he seems compelled to do whatever he can to discourage me from this whole investigation. It may as well have been an F, because unless a graduate student gets all A's, there's no way they'll be awarded their PhD. I get it that he is doing what he thinks is best, but I'm afraid that unless I get to the bottom of this, I will be haunted and have nightmares the rest of my life. It's that fear that keeps me committed to figuring this out, one way or another now, and be done with it.

I poured over maps of the rivers and found a couple of islands on each that seemed promising. The St. Croix and Chippewa Rivers were two or three hours from home, or seven hours from Madison. I decided it made sense to drive home. I got in well after dark. Mom knew I was coming, so she had a plate with supper warming in the oven. I ate, had a drink with Mom and Dad, and went to bed to another fitful night of dreams.

I got a couple hours of studying in before dawn. I smelled coffee and went downstairs to join my dad for a cup. I told him of my plan to drive along the St. Croix and Chippewa Rivers to look for islands and learn more about the early voyageur water routes through Wisconsin. I told him I had become more interested in early Wisconsin history since Dan and I did a little research at the Historical Society after I had a dream about a voyager. Dad looked at me like he thought something was fishy. It would have sounded that way to me, too. I decided to leave right away before I was compelled to go into any details about my problem. I had taken two sips of coffee when Mom came down to the kitchen to join us. She immediately started making breakfast. God, that bacon smelled delicious. Okay, my new plan was to leave right after breakfast.

While we ate, Dad tried to interest me in doing some fishing since I would be going to a couple of the best fisheries in the area. If I would stop to fish periodically, he offered to come along. I appreciated that, but declined. He loves to fish, but I am only able to tolerate it. Besides, stopping to fish would make it a longer trip and I didn't want to spend any more time than was absolutely necessary. I thanked Dad for the offer and said I planned to be back that evening.

He's probably trying to get me alone so he can ask what the hell has gotten into me. I'm not ready to go into all that with him just yet, not because I want to keep him in the dark, but because I really don't know what has gotten into me. When I know more, I'll share more.

Dad asked me what route I would be taking. I showed him my map and the islands I wanted to look at. He talked me out of going all the way down to Eau Claire because the islands in the Chippewa River there looked like oxbow islands, and based on the elevations were likely low lands or swampy. The best bet was a mid-river island just north of Jim Falls. I could get there on Highway 178. There was one promising-looking island on the St. Croix River an hour north of here. I thought I'd go there first, then south to Jim Falls, and finally circle home.

Two hundred ten miles and six hours later, I was pulling back into my parent's driveway. Another wasted effort. The "promising" island on the St. Croix had five trees, two rocks, and a stump, maybe a third of an acre in area. It was probably surveyed when the water level was low. The island north of Jim Falls wasn't right either, it didn't have the elevation or look familiar in any way.

May as well use the rest of the weekend to get my class work done. I had a lot of catch-up reading to do before I could finish my final paper.

The next morning Dad asked if I enjoyed my trip to the St. Croix. I told him it wasn't productive.

"I'm sorry to hear that, but it's not what I meant. The St. Croix is one of the most scenic and pristine rivers in the state. When I canoed there years ago, there were even old-growth pine and hemlock groves right down to the bank. Those rivers probably look today as close to what they looked two hundred years ago as any in the area. If you had a dream of that river from the eyes of a voyageur, I'm thinking that you'd have recognized it. In fact, Senator Nelson got the Wild Rivers Act passed. The Saint Croix, Namakogon, and Wolf are all on the list for that designation. I was just curious what you thought."

"Dad, they were beautiful. But frankly, I was so focused on trying to find my way to the islands I had targeted and check them out that I didn't take a moment to appreciate the surroundings. Maybe I'll have a chance to get there again for a more leisurely visit."

Dad's point was well made. I had looked past or missed a lot of beautiful and amazing things the last few months. Not just scenery, but my family, the university, and Dan. I sometimes forget how proud I felt whenever I was with him. That may explain the feelings I have of being isolated and depressed. But knowing why doesn't make me feel any better about myself.

13

On the last day of class I turned in my final paper and took the exam on our reading assignments. I know I did well on the test, but have no idea what I will get on the paper. So much for any perks for being teacher's pet.

I finally got a part-time job with the university leading tours of the campus for incoming freshmen and their families. The job was four weeks long and only two or three days a week. I had waited too long to start looking for a summer job and that was the best I could do. Dan was off to some conference in Atlanta. I wasn't on the tour schedule till next week, and with the campus rather dead during the summer I thought I'd go home. My episodes of depression were increasing. I love summers up north in Wisconsin, maybe it would be a chance to relax and get mentally energized again.

When I got home Friday afternoon, I went up to my room and immediately curled up on my bed. I started to feel myself drift toward that dark place of lethargy and thought I better do something to distract myself or I'd continue to sink emotionally. I struggled to get the energy to go downstairs Mom and Dad had just started cocktail hour as they did every Friday and Saturday at five.

"Mind if I join you?"

"Of course not, dear. We were hoping you'd come down to talk," Mom said.

"You know where the booze is. Pour yourself something," Dad added.

I made a brandy and cola and joined them on the sun porch.

"Prost," we all said simultaneously.

"Were you reading, Willa?"

"Mostly just thinking about next year and going over my notes from class. I only got a B+ for the semester. At least I got my grade up from B-. I didn't do well on my first paper."

"Why? You usually breeze through writing papers," Dad said.

"I know, but this is different. It has to do with my sensory deprivation project."

"So?"

"My problem is keeping the integrity of the science while incorporating my personal experiences. It's a balancing act."

"What does Dan suggest?"

"He's really not helping. Thinks my personal experience with the project is irrelevant. He thinks I'm crazy," I said. I was starting to lose it and could feel my eyes welling up. Shit.

"Honey, what's wrong?" Mom asked.

"Just frustration. It's hard. Can we change the subject? It's summer and I want to take a break from thinking about the project."

"Of course. I hear that Mike and Joanie's little Anna is talking up a storm already. What is she, ten-and-a-half months? Did you have a chance to see Anna when you were there?" Mom wondered.

"You sound like a gramma, Mother. I did have a chance to visit. Anna's the cutest thing!"

An hour of small talk about Dad's business, brothers Mike and Pete, Mom's garden, and two brandy and colas later, Mom went to the kitchen to check on the roast we were having for dinner. Dad went right back to the project.

"I know you're trying to take a break from thinking about school, but it might help if you talk through what's been frustrating. I'll just listen. I'm interested in what you've been learning."

"This is one of the hardest things I've ever gone through, Dad, but maybe you're right." I summarized the deprivation results, then tentatively switched gears to my dreams.

After I finished the abridged version, I said, "Dan thinks I'm crazy."

"Well, it's not every day you get a free diagnosis from a highly regarded psychologist. I'm still reeling from the diagnosis I got a few years ago from my psychologist daughter that the reason I'm a logger is due to my castration complex," Dad laughed, reminding me of a tongue-in-cheek comment I made early in my undergrad program.

"Really Dad, do you think I'm crazy?"

"Hell no. There is only one person in the world who knows what those experiences are like, and that's you. Doesn't really matter what anybody else thinks because they don't have the same information you have."

"Thanks Dad. But, does what I told you sound crazy?"

"Willa, of everyone in our family—hell, of everyone I know—you're the most logical, thoughtful and 'sane' person of the whole lot. I'll deny I said that if you ever tell your mother though," Dad chuckled.

"What advice would you give Mike and Pete about something like this?"

"Oh, probably something profound, like 'just suck it up, decide which option is best and move on.'"

"Profound indeed," I said as sarcastically as I could.

Dad laughed. "Willa, in a lot of ways it's easier for me to talk about personal matters with your brothers than with you. I hate to admit that but it's true, daughters are ... well, more complicated. So, I don't know how good my advice will be. But let's go through some of those dreams and perceptions again. Tell me about the writings you envision. Can you recall any signatures, dates, place names, or anything that would help piece things together?"

"Some. The word *fox* in French. The clothing, muskets, and other fragments of information seem seventeenth or eighteenth century. Black walnut trees on a steep hill, the river and an island seemed clear."

"Did you find anything you were looking for when you went to the Apostle Islands and last month to the Saint Croix and Chippewa Rivers?"

"Nothing, and nothing at Washington Island or Mackinac either. Mike suggested that I talk to you or Uncle Michael about possible locations because if anyone would know what I'm describing, you guys would. I didn't want to ask you about it though, because it sounds so stupid."

"It's not stupid at all. I'm not sure I'll be much help, but tell me again about that island."

After I described the wide river flowing around it, the steep rocky bluff, and the vision from both river level and from high above on a limestone ledge, Dad interrupted.

"You know, that actually sounds like a place your Uncle Michael took me just before the war. Michael wanted to try planting black walnut trees to replace a couple of 'forties' of aspen and birch we harvested. He wasn't sure what the northern range of the walnuts was and heard about a public forest on the Wisconsin side of the Mississippi River not far from Eau Claire that was loaded with mature walnuts. Black walnut wood sells at a real premium. It's used for gunstocks, high-grade veneer, one-of-a-kind furniture, that kind of thing. They really pay up for nice walnut boards.

"He took us on a trip to gather nuts to plant in peat pot containers. After they sprouted, we planted the seedlings. The trees grew fast."

"How did that work out? I don't remember any walnut trees on our properties."

"We still have about six or eight dozen growing out of the hundreds we planted. Turns out Eau Claire is about as far north as they can handle. Those that grew were damaged by every wind storm that blew through. Split trunks, broken limbs, it just wasn't profitable. Anyway, above the walnut forest was a bluff. We walked to the top and from there we saw a peninsula sticking three or four hundred feet straight up out of the Mississippi. It had a steep cliff on one side. The river didn't flow around it on both sides like you described, but it looked like it did because a tributary flowed into the Mississippi along the side of the point the bluff was on. Probably nothing, but you said you saw black walnuts and an outcropping on a bluff in a river. That sounds an awful lot like this spot. With all the areas you've explored you haven't said anything about going to the Mississippi River. That river probably has the most islands and was likely one of the most used waterway by explorers."

"Mike said the same thing. You're right, I've avoided the Mississippi because it's so long and so wide, it was just too daunting. But what you said could be really important—your description seems remarkably like what I see in the visions. How do I find the place?"

"There's a state park near there. I think I could show you the spot on a map. Hell, I'll take you there. I'm pretty sure I can still find it, it's probably an hour and a half from here. This spring has been wet and warm, so be prepared for mosquitoes."

At my urging, we left at six the next morning. I was eager to see the spot, but was skeptical. Was there really a spot like Dad described or was he just trying to patronize me? Well, if I could drive thirteen hours to check out a few islands, I could take a short drive with my dad. He insisted we take his fishing boat in case we wanted a water-side view. A twelve-foot aluminum boat with dried up minnow carcasses on the floor, anchor with muck and desiccated seaweed clinging on for dear life, and a thirty-year-old five-horse Evinrude motor. Oh God! I can even see the word "YOT" faintly visible on the bow. Peter wrote it there with a crayon when he was five or six. My dad had the boys convinced this thing was their yacht. We hooked the boat trailer to the back of Dad's pickup and were off.

As we drove, I told Dad that without some reasonable hope I didn't think I could live like this—haunted day and night, not sleeping, delusional, manic, then lethargic and depressed. "This has been a horrible experience. If there isn't a meaning to this, then I am just psychotic and that is really scary." I couldn't help myself and started crying.

"It's scary for me too, Willa. That isn't the kind of thing a parent wants to hear their daughter tell them. But I'm glad you did. Look, whatever happens, you know your mom and I will do whatever we can for you. If Dan can't help you, we'll find someone else who can. I didn't realize that what you have been going through was this bad. You never let on. Willa, you're not thinking of doing something to hurt yourself, are you?"

"Not really. But a few times things were really bad."

"Promise that if you start having those thoughts you will let me know right away. Okay?"

"Okay, I promise. But please don't share all this with Mom. She will freak out and you'll have two crazies to deal with."

"Okay, I'll keep it to myself for now."

When we were getting close, Dad stopped talking and seemed intent on trying to get his bearings. I waited for him to tell me that things had changed so much in the past thirty years that nothing looked familiar.

"There it is!" he said.

We turned into a parking lot. Ours was the only vehicle.

"Where is it?"

"Across the road. Let's go. We have a little hike. When we get there, take a moment this time to just look out at the river and appreciate the view. If it's not the place, at least you'll have seen a beautiful panoramic of the river. As I remember, it's incredible."

I agreed I would. As soon as we started up the steep trail, I recognized a familiar sight and smell from an episode in the tank—black walnut shells. I was certain it had significance. It was the end of June but littering the steep path were black half shells, the remnants of countless squirrel feasts from last fall and winter. That was a good sign and just like Dad described it. Periodically I would catch a glimpse of the Mississippi through the trees. Each time our vantage point was a bit higher but not more promising. When we reached the summit, Dad led me to a feeble wood rail, the only thing that protected the public from tumbling down the five-hundred-foot cliff.

"Just look at that view," he said.

I couldn't help but be drawn to the breathtaking bird's-eye view of the Mississippi looking south and of the bluffs on the west side of the river. It was as remarkable as Dad had said it was.

I felt Dad poke my arm. He was pointing north, up the river.

I turned in that direction and looked where he was gesturing.

My God.

"That's it! Dad, that's the island. I can't believe it!" I think I hugged him five different times.

"Are you sure? It's a peninsula, not an island. You're that sure just by looking at it?"

"Dad, I have seen that spot in visions and dreams so many times it's engrained in my mind. It's like recognizing the face of an old acquaintance in a crowd. You just know that face when you see it. The only difference is I remember it in early fall colors, and not so green as it is now. But this is it, I'm certain."

"Okay, now what?" Dad asked.

"Can we go there?"

"Well, I brought the boat so we could get a closer look from the water. But I don't think that tourists are encouraged to poke around."

"Dad, I've got to go there!"

"If you think it's that important, I suppose we can go."

We walked down the steep trail back to the truck. Dad drove us about a mile north and turned onto a dirt road. At the end of the road was a small, unimproved boat landing with just enough of a clearing to turn the truck around.

"Michael loves this spot. Claims to catch a lot of crappies and walleye just upriver from here. We only caught two small catfish when he took me fishing here years ago. This is my first time back since then."

Thanks for the fishing report, Dad, I said to myself and rolled my eyes.

We put the boat in and started downriver. When the point was in sight, it just didn't look right anymore. Doubt started to creep in.

He was guiding the boat to a small gravel spot on the north side of the point.

"Dad, can we go to the other side?"

He nodded, and turned the boat to the right and around the west side of the point. Once south of it, there wasn't a clear landing spot, but I asked Dad if we could try to land there anyway. He revved up the engine and sped us toward a wall of cattails, then turned off the engine as we glided onto a narrow spongy bog. He motioned me out. I stepped over the side of the boat and onto a weedy mat. My foot immediately sank into four inches of water. I walked a few more steps until I was on firmer footing and looked back for Dad. He had already pulled the boat up on the narrow bog, put the anchor a few feet in front of the bow, and was walking toward me.

I turned and looked up for the first time. I couldn't believe it! I had been here before! Right here! I knew exactly where I had stood before. It was just a few yards west of this spot, and I knew where the trail was up the slope.

"Do you still feel this is the place, Willa?"

"Without a doubt. This is it. I've been here before Dad. I know this place. Let's go to the ledge where I spent the night."

"The ledge *you* spent the night?"

"Yup."

"Okay. Lead the way."

I climbed through the last of the thigh-high brush and five-foot tall cattails, each with what looked like shish-kebabbed hot dogs on top. Once at the foot of the bluff I had little trouble finding the trail up. Dad followed me.

As we climbed, the trail, the sights, and smells were all familiar. It was just as I envisioned. The trail and each stone ledge we passed on the narrow path that wound its way up the south face of the bluff was exactly as I remembered. The natural limestone steps seemed worn smooth by eons of animals, Native Americans, explorers, and tourists traversing it. The vegetation today was just as it was as I envisioned. While appearing thick and lush from the bluff, up close the brush, spruce, fir, and scrub oak were dwarfed and disfigured; their roots clinging for life and fighting for scarce nutrients among the crevices, cracks, and openings in the layered rock.

The adrenalin rush I experienced when I saw the spot energized me and I easily traversed the steep two hundred yards of near vertical trail. My dad lagged behind.

Just short of the top of the bluff, I reached a rocky outcropping that looked familiar. Looking to the south, I saw the vista I had seen in my dreams many times. The Mississippi River was nearly half a mile across at that point. The steep bluffs and wooded ledges on both sides of the river and the azure sky all reflected on the water below. No houses, boats, piers, roads ... nothing. Just as it was in my visions. It was emotionally and esthetically exhilarating.

Wheezing a bit, Dad arrived several seconds later. "Dad, I'm pretty sure this is my campsite. I remember looking south down the river, cracking open and eating a handful of walnuts I had in my pocket. I was watching the Indians scour the banks downriver looking for me."

"Geez. Okay. We're at *your* campsite. Now what?"

"I left something important here. Let's look around."

We searched. Turned over rocks. Dug in the scant peat and soil pockets in the rock layers. Nothing.

"Willa, come up here," Dad called from up the bluff.

I joined him on a flat outcropping, just above the ledge I had searched.

"Look under that ledge."

My eyes took a few seconds to adjust to looking into the deep shade of the enclave in the limestone.

"What am I looking for?"

Dad pointed. Protruding from the leaf litter and loose soil was an object. The only sign that the object wasn't part of the natural landscape and did not belong was that it was a perfect circle about an inch and a half in diameter.

"That's my sidearm! I buried it there. I was going to come back and retrieve it later." Just like the name on the map served as a catalyst for disjointed memories and visions I've been having, so was the sight of the butt of the handle of that gun. I knew what it looked like before I dug it up. I knew there were other things placed there, too. I remember being frightened, cold, and alone. This place provided the first concrete clue in my search for answers. I felt so ... so not crazy any more.

I knelt and carefully dug the leaves, twigs, limestone chips, and cool black soil from around the object and lifted it out. Even in the deep shadow of the damp v-shaped cave, I could see the badly rusted and weathered, but unmistakable remains of a flintlock pistol. I held it in my hands briefly, then reverently passed it to my dad.

He took it and looked at it, looked at me. "Willa, this is remarkable. What else did you leave here?"

"Let's find out."

We continued to carefully push the dirt, leaves, and twigs aside and look for artifacts.

A foot or two from the pistol, I found something else buried. It was deeper and took a little digging to get it out. It looked like a leather bag. I took it out into the light and sat next to Dad. We slowly peeled away the stiff and brittle black remnants of a leather flap.

"You know Willa, this is an archeological site. These are artifacts that should be excavated by specialists. We could destroy something historically valuable. Maybe we already have. Shouldn't we just leave this as it is and let the park service know?"

"No way, Dad! Please, I've got to know what's here. This is my chance to prove that I'm not crazy. I've got to get to the bottom of this. Come on, don't wuss out on me, Dad."

"Okay, but we go carefully, slowly, and leave the site as close to how we found it as possible. Okay?"

"Okay."

I continued to peel off the crusted remains of what once had been a satchel. Inside were cloth fragments, "My shirt and blanket." The remnants of the blanket, which had not yet been eaten by moths or chewed away by mice and weather, was stained by tannin leaching from the soil making it various shades of blacks and browns. Clear eight-inch wide stripes were visible. Unfolding the blanket, the original colors of red, beige, and green were discernable. In one of the corners, exposed for the first time in two hundred and fifty years, were three, four-inch black lines stitched into the fabric.

"What is that, Willa?"

"This was a trade blanket. See those three lines? That means it was intended to be exchanged for three beaver pelts from the Indian trade partners. I used it right here. I remember pulling it over my shoulders, holding it together with my hands at my chest as I sat in this cave looking out at the fading light of dusk flicker on the river below. I remember sitting here Dad, thinking that may have been the last sunset I'd ever see. I was in grave danger. The Indians that were patrolling the river were looking for me. That's why I didn't build a fire. I didn't want to give away my location. That's why I left these things here, to travel as light as possible."

I continued to unwrap the blanket. Inside were the fragments of the tightly woven course-linen of my shirt. The outside folds were dark brown with frayed edges and holes. The outer fabric broke as I unfolded it. Inside, the cloth was lighter in color, but still not the natural light sallow color of the linen as I remembered it. The clam shell buttons, laying on the inside of the folded shirt, seemed just as I remembered them, although the thread that bound them to the shirt had disintegrated long ago.

At the very bottom of the bag was a small glass bottle with a wooden stopper, empty except for blackened sides. Next to it were three sticks. "It's my ink and pens. See, the two larger sticks are cut diagonally on the tip and have a little ridge all the way up, those were the feathers of the quill. The smallest one is a pen made from the hollow leg bone of a crane. It has the same diagonal point." Holding up the biggest piece of a small broken clay bowl where a broken-off stem had been attached, "Here's my pipe."

Dad sat down next to me. I unwrapped the last item. It appeared to be in good condition, having been protected by the satchel and wrapped in the shirt. It looked like a book. I pulled away the disintegrating strap that used to bind the leather flaps shut. Slowly and gently opening the stiff pages, we saw a faint handwritten page of notes. Somehow I knew the pages of parchment were the ones I had so clearly envisioned myself writing upon. I could see my hand holding a pen, dipping it into the ink jar and writing. I remember making ink out of charcoal soot, water, and glue from boiled deer hides. The writing was barely legible, and the pages were disfigured with eaten edges, worm holes, and stains. The first entry was dated *octobre 1711.*

"What language is that, Willa?"

"French."

"Can you read any of it?"

"I can read all of it."

"I didn't know you could read French."

"I can't, but Dad, I can read this, because it's like I wrote it."

On a limestone ledge high above the Mississippi River, on that sunny summer day, I sat with my dad and began reading the first entries. I read the translated words aloud. It didn't matter that many of the entries were too faded and stained beyond legibility. I knew what was written. I read it with excitement and without pause. Enraptured, Dad listened intently.

2 octobre 1711
je François Renaulti 1st Le Fusilier Company 14 de la Marines faire ma premiere entrée de journal ...
    "His name is François Renaulti. He is a member of the First Fusilier Company Fourteen of the marines and is making his first entry in the journal. He says he is keeping a journal because he promised his lady friend, Shiree, that he would. She worries. François had been wounded in the side two years before while he was a soldier at the Battle of Oudenaarde.

    "That's what I had a dream about, Dad! I dreamt I was wounded in the left side while crossing a bridge during a battle. That had to have been a battle during the Spanish War of Succession! That war was still going on in 1712. He fought in Europe, got wounded, recovered, and then got deployed to Canada. This is who I have been channeling. This is the guy! There is no doubt."

    I continued to read and translate the journal for my dad.

    "If he was unable to return to Bayonne himself, he intended to send her the journal so she would know he was okay. Dad, this is weird. As I read this, certain words trigger vivid memories and images. When I read Bayonne, I saw rolling arid hills and two rivers. A farm field of pepper plants. The sight of the plants stimulates a taste in my mouth of peppers. Bayonne is his hometown."

    "How do you know what you're seeing and remembering aren't just convoluted fragments of your own dreams?"

    "I don't really know, Dad. But it is so real, so familiar. Let's see what's next."

9 octobre 1711
    "His marine company is being sent to Canada to bolster defenses against English attacks, but he doesn't know

much about their orders. They are sailing through a storm. He's been seasick and not eating."

21 octobre 1711

"He is complaining about the putrid water but at least the troops receive two pints of wine each day with their rations. He isn't seasick from the constant rocking any more but has been having stomach issues. He says this isn't worth the twelve livres he gets paid a month. I don't know how much a livre is, but he thinks it's a pittance.

"Seems like he's getting philosophical now. Evidently there are only three social classes in France: those who work, the lowest class or the bourgeois, those who pray, the Jesuits, and those who fight. They are the nobility. François thinks the only way to move up in society is to distinguish himself as a soldier. His family owns land but having uncles and five brothers they will all be condemned to be bourgeois forever. Then he talks about enjoying Descartes work."

"Willa, do you know what he's talking about?"

"Yes, I think so. It was customary in France for fathers to divide their farms among their sons. After each generation the size of the parcels bequeathed to each son got smaller and smaller. He felt his parcel was too meager and would condemn him and his heirs to progressively lower and lower social status within the working class. He credits Descartes' philosophy on doubt and certainty for guiding his decision to let his brothers divide his land while he gambles that he can elevate his status as a soldier and voyageur. That's what seems to have guided him here. He wanted to impress Shiree and earn the social status of her family. He must have figured that was the only way she'd marry him."

"You got all that from a journal entry?"

"Like I said, some of the entries seem to trigger memories. I don't know how they got there, but they seem real. It's like déjà vu except I don't just feel like I have seen this before, I remember everything about it.

"Reading his words must stimulate my memory. The

same thing happened when I saw this spot and when Dan and I went to the archives and found an old map. It just flows. Hopefully we will run across something that we can do a fact check on to see if this stream of information I've been getting is real or just the product of fantasy. I sure hope this all checks out. Otherwise Dan will be even more convinced this is all a big delusion. But, so far as I can tell, the writing, my memories, and the historical record all jive."

26 octobre 1711
Companies 1–10 deployed to Porte Royale. Arcadian may be lost. English cochons!

"He got briefed on their mission. His Company and three others were deployed from France to reinforce the French Territory in Canada against the English. A French fort at Port Royale and the territory of Arcadian were under siege by the English and their Indian allies. Evidently, they were originally going to reinforce Port Royale, but they received news that it fell when they made a port of call in Newfoundland and got a change of orders. His Company would be under General Renard Dubuisson's command in Montreal. The plan is to help build fortifications there and then serve as reinforcements with the general when he assumes control of Fort Pontchartrain du Detroit. The plan is to give a show of strength to the Indians to bolster alliances and ultimately bring the fight to the English. He says that his Company's spirits are high and they are eager to sail and to fight.

4 novembre 1711
We entered the narrows of LeFleuve St. Laurent last night. I feel stronger.

"He's complaining about how retched the three weeks on the ship were, but they're finally in the St. Lawrence River and getting close to their destination. They are on alert since they saw an English ship scuttled on the rocks in the river. At their first port of call after reaching French territory, and when they learned that all of Arcadian was lost, they were also informed that there had been an ill-fated English attempt earlier in the year to attack Quebec. It seems the English lost three ships to a storm, but they weren't sure if they were still in the area.

"Now he's complaining about the king. Evidently, he overheard the officers talking and they think that the king is too preoccupied with who will be attending his *coucher* and his endless 'quest for fuel for his vanity' than he is in military strategy for New France." I paused.

"That sounds like he's not very impressed with his king," Dad said.

"He isn't. Most of the officers and soldiers aren't either. It seems to them that good generals like SeBastian de Vauban and Duc deVendome are being replaced by court favorites who receive their commission not on merit but on how much they are willing to kiss the king's ass. That really pisses off the rank and file. The king announced that he would take a lead role in directing the military effort in the War of Spanish Succession, but the soldiers think he is only leading when there is a siege or a review, so he can ride among the troops and look splendid but vanish when there is any danger or real action."

"What does *coucher* mean?"

"Louis required his court and ministers to be in attendance, as though it was a privilege for them, to be present when the King got dressed, peed, ate, and *coucher*, got ready for bed. If you missed one of those action-packed episodes, it could really hurt your career."

As I read passage after passage aloud, I kept thinking that I couldn't wait to share this with Dan. He won't believe it. I'm looking at the 250-year-old journal of the dead guy who has been in my head. This is irrefutable evidence that my dreams aren't delusions. This has to convince him that I'm not a nut case.

8 novembre 1711
We arrived at Montreal. Good riddance to that ship.

"They arrived at Montreal. There is work in progress constructing a stone fortress around the city. With the addition of the men in his company he thinks it will be done by the end of the year and hopes the English don't attack the city until after they finish. His barracks have dirt floors, no windows, and deer hides for a door. It is adjacent to Sainte Anne de Bellevue Church and the *grande Chateau Ramezay*, which, along with the Decarie Chateau. is used for officer quarters. He says that there are to be no dirt floors for the officers."

15 novembre 1711

"After they finished morning drills and a few hours of stone work on the walls, his grenadier, Beloit, told the troops of their orders. His fusilier company, led by General Dubuisson, is to travel to Ponchartrain in a couple of weeks so Dubuisson can replace General Cadillac. Evidently the Jesuits had complained to the governor that General Cadillac had been unlawfully using brandy and guns to win the favor of the local Indians. The governor was irate and ordered Cadillac out.

13 decembre 1711

"Before leaving for Ponchartrain, they received orders to march north to intercept an English incursion from Hudson Bay. The *la reine cochon*? ... Dad, that means *the pig queen*. He's demeaning Queen Anne of England. Earlier he called the English 'pigs.' He cursed Etienne Brulé."

"Who was Brulé? Why curse him for the English incursion?"

"Brulé became a traitor and helped the English enter the beaver trade in Canada at Hudson Bay. Brulé was a Couriers de Bois, which was an independent entrepreneurial French-Canadian who kept some of the profit from their trapping and trading. The governor of New France forbade independent fur trading. Brulé traded for furs anyway, and used brandy for trading with the Indians, and that was prohibited. The governor confiscated his hundreds of beaver pelts when he returned to Montreal. Brulé was pissed and defected to the English. All this happened years before François arrived, but it must have still been talked about in Montreal when he got there."

"I didn't know you were this interested in history, or so well read, Willa."

"Dad, I'm not. I hated every history class I ever took. But like I said, I just know this stuff. I don't know how, I just do. I did some research and poked around at the library and a couple of museums a little. I learned some things but most of the information just confirmed what I already knew. It seems that if François knew it, I know it now."

15 decembre 1711

"Evidently they turned back from trying to intercept the English, the snow was too deep. Only the Metis scouts pressed on."

"Who are the 'Metis'?"

"I think François knew them as mixed blood, the product of marriages between Frenchmen and Indian women. This was a mutually beneficial practice. So much so that in southern Canada, the Metis came to be the dominant Indian presence. For voyageurs these marriages ensured good relationship with a tribe so they would have a supply of furs and safe travel, and for the Indians it solidified a partner in lucrative trade. The Indians really valued the iron tools, pots, and axes, which were legal, but they also were eager to get brandy and guns. Although it was illegal to trade those things with the Indians, some traders did. There were a lot of rivalries and alliances between the Indian tribes, which made establishing trading partners tricky business. At the Great Meeting of Tribes in Montreal, someone told François that there were over thirty different Indian tribes represented."

"Willa, I didn't think there were even thirty tribes in all of North America."

"That's one of the reasons making treaties and alliances was so complicated. It wasn't just a matter of which tribes were willing to trade with France and fight the British, but assuaging long held grudges, or perceived indignities."

25 decembre 1711

"François celebrated Christmas Mass and drank 'much of the Jesuits' wine' at the party afterward, even though it was intended for the officers and not the fusiliers like him."

3 janvier 1712

"He's bored. It's too cold and there's too much snow for drills or to spend much time outside his barracks. They are playing cards and trying to stay as close to the fire pit as they can. The loser at cards has to bring in more firewood. He's making friends with a Paul Dupre. Dupre has been in Montreal since 1708, and has been helping François understand the geography, the Indian tribe alliances, and how the war there differs from the fighting François experienced in the 'gentleman's war' in Europe. Dupre acknowledged that the fighting in Europe can be brutal, but told François that war here is without rules. He called it 'win or die' warfare. The English haven't sent many regular troops to America yet. They have relied on the colonists to defend themselves with the help of Indian allies. The French are trying to make up for the lack of colonists to occupy territory by dispatching troops and building forts.

"France kept a monopoly on land ownership and trade for the 'Company of the Colony of Canada.' This practice didn't encourage colonization. Why risk the arduous trip and brutality of the on-going war without the possibility of reward? For the most part, the only French colonists are former soldiers and voyageurs who have married Indian wives and some officers who brought their families with them. Instead, the French courted alliances with the Indians using trade as an incentive to remain friendly with the French.

"Dupre plans to accompany Le Moyne d'Iberville on an expedition west, then south.

"It seems that the king sent soldiers to establish a settlement midway between New Orleans and Montreal, at Biloxi in 1699. The plan was to expand the existing posts at Kaskaskira, Cahokia, and Vincennes in the Illinwek Territory, which was Illinois. That's when the post at Michilimackinac was strengthened and General Cadillac received royal permission to found Fort Pontchartrain."

"That's Detroit, isn't it Willa?"

"Yup. Fort Pontchartrain du Detroit. Cadillac was eventually booted out of the fort he financed and had built because he was running it to enrich himself. The king and governor only wanted themselves enriched. That's when François came to the fort. Cadillac was 'promoted' to Mobile to get him out of the way. His fort was taken over by Dubuisson. D'Iberville's orders were to make the lower Mississippi River region southern New France. Dupre told François that there were too few settlers willing to colonize around the forts. No one wanted to volunteer without the promise of land or good pay. François said Dupre laughed, *Roi Soleil* will have no Protestants in France—*Un roi, une loi, une foi!* Dad, I knew that! One king, one law, one faith! That's what that says. I told Dan, but he didn't believe it. That isn't what the history book said, so he said it couldn't be right! I can't wait to read this to him. It was the Edict of Fountainebleau. Louis the Fourteenth eliminated religious freedom in France. Hundreds of thousands of French Protestants, mostly Huguenots, fled to England and Holland, and then to America. Years later they were the colonists fighting for the English against the French during that period. That decision really came around to bite the French."

I continued to translate and read the journal aloud.

"It seems that Dupre enlisted because he was promised a promotion, higher pay, and a possible govenorship of the Carolinians' settlements once they captured the territory. D'Iberville, Dupre, and 110 troops were to route the English

Carolinians, take Spanish Pensacola, and finally New York. All would become part of New France.

"Dupre called it a *'Grande Plan,* pitiful results.' They made it to Cuba for supplies. There, D'Iberville and dozens of men died of the yellow fever. Dupre and the remaining troops returned to France. That's when he was ordered to Montreal to reinforce the garrison and help construct the stone fortifications. He got there a couple of years before François."

28 février 1712

"An Ottawa runner arrived and told François' commander of a Fox raiding party of five hundred warriors joining the main camp near the fort. Dad, I saw that word in one of the visions I had in the tank. I saw my handwriting *Les Renards!* This must have been important to François, probably because the Fox were antagonists and not to be trusted. Small camps of friendly tribes, the Ottawas and Hurons, were nearby. The tribes had been called together by General Cadillac to discuss a strategy to repel the Iroquois and English and most of the Ottawa and Huron warriors were fighting the Iroquois in the east. The Fox were not."

9 mars 1712
Ojibwae party arrived by canoe.

"Indian allies alerted Dubuisson that the Fox were grouping for an attack on Pontchartrain. They learned of the change in commanders planned for Pontchartrain and with the men of the other tribes fighting far to the west, they planned to attack the fort and other tribes late that spring."

21 mars 1712

"They received orders to prepare to accompany Dubuisson to Ponchartrain."

7 avril 1712

"There was finally a warm spell, so they sailed that morning. Three small ships."

12 avril 1712

"They arrived at dusk.

"Fort Pontchartrain is smaller than he expected, about one arpent square, that's about 190 feet. There were only twenty-nine troops before he arrived, but with his unit the garrison is now at forty. He is assigned to the barracks next to the ice house. It has a hard-packed dirt floor and bark roof. There is one small window covered with a deer skin scraped thin, so it would let in a little light."

14 avril 1712

"General Cadillac transferred his command to General Dubuisson in a short ceremony. He left with a squad of grenadiers, two of the officers' wives, and two wounded voyageurs with their furs. Cadillac is on his way to Montreal, then on to Mobile. Evidently, Cadillac pissed off some higher ups, but he had enough allies in Quebec to be given a new command and not be sent back to Paris to answer to the king for ignoring the edict against self-dealing."

15 avril 1712

"Two voyageurs returned and claimed they were ambushed. Seven in the party were killed. Their canoes were swarmed by Fox warriors. The two survivors were in the lead canoe and were able to paddle to safety despite their wounds. They made it to the fort with about half of their load of furs. They were directed to return to Montreal because the governor wanted the furs and their information about the Fox. The governor was also interested in any information he could get on Sioux activity in the west, and about a guy named Bourgnout. Dupre told François that Bourgnout deserted his post after being disciplined. Ojibwas claim they heard that Bourgnout is exploring and mapping the river system west of the Mississippi. The governor wants that land claimed for New France. Knowing whether the Sioux are hostile and getting maps of the area would be helpful in the governor's attempt to expand the French territory west."

17 avril 1712

"Soon after his unit arrived, they saw the glow of the Fox campfires on the night skyline. The other tribes' campfires were faint and barely visible. It seems clear to the Indian allies that the Fox are massing near the fort with the intention to attack and the allies tell François that his unit arrived none too soon."

19 avril 1712

"The initial attack was repulsed. A dozen warriors were killed.

"Two casualties in the fort. The Ottawa said there were at least thirteen hundred Fox warriors and their women and children. It seemed that with the change in fort leadership and many of the Huron and Ottawa warriors off fighting elsewhere, the Fox intended to use this opportunity to destroy the fort and take over the territory."

23 avril 1712

"There are no attacks for two days."

1 mai 1712

"After the attack that morning, they inventoried shot, powder, and provisions. They were still in good supply, but had less each day. The Fox patrolling the harbor would prevent resupply.

"The fort had seven casualties, four dead."

4 mai 1712

"François says there was whooping all night from the Fox camp, and he didn't get much sleep.

"Beginning at dawn there were several fierce attacks during the day, but quieted by nightfall."

9 mai 1712

"The attack that night almost breached their two-toist's log walls. That's about twelve feet, Dad. Three Fox warriors were killed inside the fort. The fort lost six men before the Fox fled. Another week or two of this and he doesn't think they will be able to repel them."

12 mai 1712

"Whooping again that night, but no attack today."

13 mai 1712

"Hundreds of Indians appeared north and west of the fort. They were the returning Ottawas and Hurons.

"Seven of their chiefs sat with the general and his officers for two hours.

"François' grenadier told him the chiefs said their returning warriors had the Fox pinned between the fort and their two armies. They planned to attack them the next day."

15 mai 1712

"Since they arrived the French Indian allies had been attacking the Fox camp relentlessly.

"The Fox were trying to negotiate a retreat for their women and children. They would leave the area and move west.

"Sporadic musket fire."

16 mai 1712

"The Fox chiefs came to the fort and said they would agree to lay down their arms for their safe passage west.

"The Ottawa chiefs adamantly rejected the offer. They want to rid their territory of the Fox and are intent on killing every Fox they can. The Huron's are less bent on destroying the Fox because their territory is farther east and the Fox have been less of a problem. Father Charles protests killing of innocents. The general agreed to the terms offered by the Fox. The Ottawa's are outraged and seek *effusion de sang* ..."

"Effusion what? I can follow most of what you're reading Willa, but I don't understand that."

"That means *much blood.* Wars between the Fox and Ottawa have been on again off again for decades. The Ottawa saw a chance to annihilate the Fox once and for all. The Fox camp has been fortified, but is surrounded. The Huron's are an eastern tribe clashing mostly with the Iroquois. They don't share the Ottawa's hate for the Fox. The Fox knew their tribe would be decimated for decades if their camp was overrun and women and children weren't spared. Instead, the Fox agreed to have their warriors go to an open plain called Grosse Pointe and lay down their arms. They would do this for the assurance of safe passage west, into Wisconsin. That's Ottawa territory, too, and they're pissed about it."

17 mai 1712

"As they agreed, the Fox warriors assembled at Grosse Pointe just north of the fort. They put their muskets, axes, and bows in piles. Once they had laid down their arms, the Ottawa attacked. A massacre ensued ..."

"That doesn't sound like it turned out so good for the Fox."

"No, it sure doesn't. As the Fox warriors headed back toward their camp, the Ottawa and Huron attacked them on two sides. Without arms, hundreds of Fox warriors trying to get back to their camp were slaughtered, the wounded hatcheted.

"The attack turned toward the Fox camp. Ottawa and Huron swarmed the camp. The Fox were able to offer some resistance with arms they had hidden in their camp that weren't brought to Grosse Pointe. The remaining Fox fled west with the Ottawa in pursuit."

"What did François and the French do?"

"Nothing. The general had agreed to terms and honored them. But the Jesuits were enraged that the attack was merciless and many of the Fox women and children were caught and enslaved or killed. Any warriors that were wounded were killed. The general was in a delicate spot. The Jesuits had a lot of political clout with the king, so the general didn't want to upset the Jesuits, and since the Ottawa were an important ally against the British, he didn't want to alienate them, either. He was between the proverbial rock and a hard place. He chose to just sit still for the time being."

23 mai 1712

"The Indian allies made sure the Fox would not be causing mischief again. They continued to pursue and attack the Fox as they fled all the way back to their encampment west of Lake Mishouakin.

"The surviving Fox were on the move en masse. Ottawa and Huron were in pursuit. General Dubuisson felt he had given the allied tribes ample opportunity to exact revenge on the Fox. There was talk that François and a small company of troops would be ordered to accompany a Jesuit priest to follow the allied tribes. The Jesuits had lobbied to let them try to stem further slaughter. François' grenadier said Dubuisson wouldn't send troops out of the fort until he got reinforcements because the English and their Iroquois friends were causing trouble just to the east."

4 juin 1712

"Several Ojebwa came to the fort and reported that they found the bodies of the seven voyageurs killed in the ambush François first heard about from the two survivors. The bodies were dismembered and *mangé*."

"What is *mangé*?"

"Eaten, Dad."

"Geez. I didn't know cannibalism was an Indian custom."

"It was, particularly captured enemies. It was considered a way to honor the strength and courage of your

84

adversary. Burning captives alive, torture, and taking trophies like scalps was common during Queen Anne's War and persisted throughout all the French and English Wars in North America."

"Willa, did you ever read *Last of the Mohicans*?"

"No, I never had it assigned, and I don't usually choose historical stuff for pleasure reading," I said.

"Well, it's a great book. Although the setting was forty years later than François' time, there are a lot of similarities, but no mention of cannibalism during the French and Indian War."

"François didn't think it was commonplace, but there were a couple of other episodes he knew about. One occurred at Coulee Grou where three captured settlers were cannibalized, and again following the massacre at Lactine," I said.

"I've never heard of either of those."

"At Lactine, the Iroquois crossed the St. Lawrence River and attacked a farming settlement a few miles west of Montreal. The Iroquois attacked with 1500 warriors and the French were reluctant to move troops out of their forts to counterattack a force that large. The entire area would've been vulnerable if they failed to destroy the Iroquois. Eventually the Iroquois moved back across the St. Lawrence with dozens of captives. Several captured men were burned alive and eaten while the women and children captives watched. It was all pretty grisly."

"What about the women and children?"

"They were essentially treated as slaves and either escaped, died, or were assimilated into the tribe. European diseases and warfare decimated the population of every tribe in the region. Kidnapping was a means of bolstering their numbers. Tribal size meant survival. The larger the tribe the less likely others would try to take their territory, and larger tribes were able to negotiate more effectively with the French and English. That's how the Iroquois flourished. They negotiated or bullied other tribes into alliances and used their superior numbers and aggressiveness to conquer and take captives from those who resisted. The Iroquois chose the English as allies, not the other way around."

"So why didn't they side with the French?"

"The Iroquois lost respect for the French at Lactine. Not only did the French leave the farmers poorly protected, the Iroquois thought of them as cowards for not attacking and driving them out, and they didn't think the French could beat the English. They were right. But being on the winning side didn't help them much in the long run though."

"Didn't the French ever retaliate against the Iroquois for that massacre?"

"They did. First against the Iroquois at the Battle of Two Mountains, when a couple dozen French Couriers de Bois killed twenty Iroquois not far from Montreal. But because they blamed the English for encouraging the Lactine attack and for providing the muskets, they retaliated against English colonists near Schenectady. The French and Indian allies attacked at night during a snowstorm. They caught the settlement completely off guard. Killed scores—anyone they could. The ones who were able to escape into the woods tried to make it to the fort nearby. But because they were still in their night clothes, many froze to death. The brutality of the war scared the hell out of François. He was a 'grunt' in the French army in Europe, but for the most part they were still using gentlemen rules of warfare. If you were captured, often they would just make you swear that you would not return to fight again, take your weapon, and let you go. Officers were held for ransom or traded for their own captured officers. Massacres, torture, and butchering civilians occurred, but were the exception. I'm sure he was shocked by the stories he heard and by what he saw of the warfare in North America, because I experienced his fear and panic in my dreams."

11 juin 1712

"Louis de la Porte de Louvigny arrived with a hundred

men. François hadn't heard why, but he and Dupre joked that they didn't come to enjoy accommodations in the fort.

"It turns out they were there to speed up the rebuilding of Sainte Anne's Church.

"Father Charles repeatedly asked Dubuisson to let him travel west. He feared unnecessary slaughter was occurring at the Fox stronghold, and he wanted to try to stop it and to convert as many heathens as he could. That, François said, was the Jesuit solution to every Indian problem. Dubuisson finally agreed to let Father Charles go and accompany troops being sent to join the siege of the Fox refuge. The governor wanted a French presence deeper into the western territory. But instead of staying at the siege, Father Charles was ordered to organize a party to travel to Fort Sainte Antoine, rebuild it and use it as a base. From there explore, map, and mark territory with French territory monuments; and Father Charles could convert all the new Christians he can. Those who accompanied the Father would be rewarded with large tracks of land and trading rights in the territory they marked. This would expand New France and would be useful in any future territory conflicts with the Spanish and English."

"Where was Fort Sainte Antoine, Willa?"

"I don't know where. I only know it was built by a guy named Perrot twenty or so years before François' expedition."

"Willa, that has to be near Perrot Park and that is about where we are. That's where your friend François' was headed. This is incredible!" Dad said.

"Dad, I knew this. I saw it in visions and nightmares. These are my 'delusions.' I'm so excited. I can't wait to show Dan."

I hugged Dad.

"Willa, what an incredible find. It's hard to believe."

19 juin 1712

"François volunteered to accompany Father Charles to

the western territory. He was accepted, and delighted with his good fortune. How else could a lowly fusilier become a land baron? He would join Father Charles as a Couriers de Bois, like Perrot. Perrot is a legend in Quebec among voyageurs but out of favor with the governor. Perrot had a small fortune in furs destroyed in a Fox raid, and despite his value to France, was never compensated with a title, land, or pension. When François wrote, this Perrot was living out his old age as a poor man writing his memoirs. François, however, intended to return to France and Shiree a rich man, no longer bourgeois, but perhaps as an officer and land baron. She would be proud to marry him and hopefully François would get her father's blessing.

"The elimination of the Fox threat made his journey possible. The Fox had been causing problems for years along the water routes and for the French and their Indian allies. The Fox even tried to stop all the French canoes traveling west of the portage and charged tolls. While there were still villages of Fox all the way to the Mississippi, the main body was holed up and under siege.

"He understood that he must remain a fusilier in the fight against the Fox and, for the time being, to protect Father Charles on the journey. Once the group made it to Fort Antoine, he and two of the other fusiliers would travel west to mark and claim territory. He prayed that he would return safely and as a rich man, God willing."

21 juin 1712

"Pierre DeNiau has become a friend to François. DeNiau was in Montreal for three years after returning from a voyage west of Lake Mishouakin. He fought the Iroqois at Lactine. François had heard of that massacre and the atrocities but was shocked when DeNiau told him that six Frenchmen captured at Lactine were burned alive and eaten while the other captives watched. When François said he told DeNiau that he was stunned that the Indians were capable of such savagery, DeNiau wanted to know how that was different from Magdeburg, or when the king ordered the burning of Jews at the stake, or the garroting of deserters and displaying their heads on pikes like the governor often did?"

Dad interrupted, "Willa, what is Magdaburg?"

"I'm not sure exactly. François only seemed to know that before he was born and during the religious wars early in the seventeenth century there was a siege of the town of Magdeburg. The Catholic army finally overwhelmed the mostly Protestant defenders and massacred them. Despite the fact that the city contained both Catholics and Protestants, the Catholic general said something to the effect, 'Kill them all, God will sort out his own' and his soldiers did just that, slaughtering virtually the entire population of the city. DeNiau told other stories of the savagery of the wars and of the Indians, but called them 'little fish' compared to the scale of what happened in Europe. One of those small-scale episodes had something to do with Etienne Brulé. He's the same guy François mentioned earlier as a traitor for helping the British. It seems the Huron's had adopted Brulé into their tribe. When Brulé fled authorities after betraying the French, he tried to rejoin the Huron. But the Huron were French allies and they felt dishonored by Brulé's deceptions, so they burned him alive on a spit and ate him."

25 juin 1712

"They followed the Fox Indians' trail back across Lake Mishouakin. Crossing the expanse in a flotilla of *bateauxes* and large Ottawa canoes. *Bateauxes* are large-bowed, wide, sturdy, stable rowboats of French design."

29 juin 1712

"They met up with their Indian allies who had the Fox stronghold surrounded. The Fox had retreated to an island near Lake Butte des Morts. The Ho-Chunks joined the attack and told François that most of the Fox from Ho-Chunk and Ojibwa territory left their camps to help reinforce the other Fox holed up here. Evidently, they are well-provisioned with water, rice, and fowl and could hold out indefinitely. With the siege likely to take many months, and the Indian allies eager to see the fighting through, Father Charles received orders to travel west. François was to accompany him."

1 juillet 1712

"After their brief stay at Lake Butte des Morts, Father Charles' expedition set out. It consisted of two groups. One, led by mapmaker Guillaume de L'Isle and François' friends, Pierre DeNiau and Joseph Parant, was to begin mapping the western territory. The second group of Jean LeFay, LaBlanc, François, and a Metis guide named Stone Axe would accompany Father Charles on his quest to convert Indian souls. The groups would travel together until they reached Fort Sainte Nichole. There they would stay for a few days, do some repairs, and then split up before rendezvousing in September at Fort Sainte Antoine. Then, de L'Isle's group would begin the second phase of their mission, which was to continue mapping the region and search for Bourgnout, the deserter that François mentioned earlier. Father Charles' would accompany L'Isle from there and continue to convert souls of the Ho-Chunk and any remaining scattered bands of Fox they encountered. François and two other soldiers were to set out with some trade goods and copper plaques with the king's insignia to serve as territory markers to claim the land. François' role would change from soldier protecting Father Charles to Couriers de Bois. At that point he would travel west to mark and claim new territory for France. François was told he and the others would be rewarded with a promotion, land, or fur trading opportunities with Indian tribes with whom they negotiated. This was the opportunity that brought François on the expedition."

5 juillet 1712

"They were traveling in five canoes and carried axe heads, kettles, and blankets to re-establish Fort Sainte Antoine as a trading site. François says that the metal plates engraved with the mark of Louis the Fourteenth and the French cross that he would use to claim new territory are the most valuable items they are carrying, at least to him. Once the fort is repaired, it will be his job to go west into unexplored territory and place the markers.

"He preferred traveling in a *bateaux,* but they are too heavy to portage. They brought provisions for ten days ... They camped at the portage of 'Riviere aux Renard' from Butte des Morts and traveled west toward Fort Sainte Nichole.

"Dad, I know what François is writing, but my geography is too weak to know exactly where he is talking about. I assume it has something to do with the Mississippi River since Dan and I saw Fort Sainte Nichole on one of the old maps we found in the archives."

"I think so, too. From what you said you've read, if the Fox Indians are the *Renard,* then the *Riviere Renard* might be the Fox River. Butte des Morts is at Lake Winnebago. You remember, whenever we'd cross that bridge in Oshkosh your brothers would laugh and read the sign 'Lake Butt.' So from what I can tell, he is pretty clearly traveling from Lake Winnebago to what is now the city of Portage, crossing over land to the Wisconsin River and on to the Mississippi. That may have been the route first taken by Joliet or Marquette, and was an important portage. It would make sense that François' group would already know of that passage."

"That's sounds pretty logical. I should have been able to figure that out."

"Willa, are you going to read the entire journal here?"

I paged ahead to see how much was left. "No, there are at least thirty pages to go. We should probably start heading back to the truck. But I've got to take the journal with me to finish reading it, take notes and show it to Dan. I know I violated an archeological site, and taking the journal is illegal, but Dad, I need to study it. There has to be some information here that will be useful if I'm going to resolve this. The fact that we found this stuff based on my visions really makes me feel like maybe I'm not crazy after all. I will leave the other stuff as we found them, and once I've gone through the journal carefully, I will either return it here or turn it over to the appropriate person or authorities."

"I don't like you taking it. But you're the one with the nightmares or whatever, and I want you to be okay. If this helps you then I'm for it. My daughter comes first."

"Thanks, Dad."

I buried the flintlock sidearm and larger satchel with the blanket and shirt where we found them and led Dad back down the trail to our boat. There were so many thoughts going through my mind, I didn't realize we were back at the launch site until Dad shouted for me to take the tie line and jump on shore.

We loaded the boat back on the trailer and started home. I continued reading all the way home. When I came across something that I thought Dad would be interested in, I read it out loud.

6 juillet 1712

"François is complaining that he aches of paddling. Fourteen hours on the river with stops for a pipe every hour or two. He can't sleep on his side because his shoulders are too sore to lie on them. Blisters on his hands throb. He says they must have portaged or pulled the canoe through twenty rapids that day. None of that seemed to affect Stone Axe."

8 juillet 1712

"They ate *menomonie* and sturgeon that they shot while it swam in the river shallows. He wrote that he's too exhausted to add more ..."

"Eating *menomonie*. Don't tell me he was a cannibal, too!"

"No, Dad. Menomonie *is* the name of an Indian tribe, but in this case he is using the Indian word for wild rice, which is also *menomonie*."

10 juillet 1712

"They aren't seeing much game and are in Ho-Chunk territory. François wrote that he remembered from an old Perrot report he read in Montreal that the Ho-Chunk numbers had already fallen dramatically just two years after his first visit."

24 juillet 1712

"They reached the Mississippi and the site of Fort Sainte Nichole. He's pretty clearly disappointed, and wrote, 'This is not a fort! It's a hovel surrounded by gaping, leaning and missing log walls. It is twenty-five paces square and offers little protection. If this is what Fort Sainte Antoine is like we will have much work to do when we arrive.'"

30 juillet 1712

"The next day the groups split up. Guillaume de L'Isle's group went north and Father Charles' group south in search of Ho-Chunk villages. They planned to meet up again at Fort Sainte Antoine in September."

3 Août 1712

"They reached a Ho-Chunk village and got a very cool welcome. François described them as a tall people. He wrote that he is five feet four inches, taller than many of his comrades, but he was nearly a head shorter than most Ho-Chunk men. The Ho-Chunk language is Sioux, the same as the Winnebago. The village consists of thirty oval bark houses with one or two families in each. Bison and deer skins are stretched between poles in the center of the village."

9 Août 1712

"Father Charles got his first converts. Three village women. Two are widows, and one badly crippled by disease. Father Charles tried to hide his disappointment and asked one of the converts why they haven't seen more Ho-Chunk villages along the rivers. They told him that the loss of so many from strange diseases, which they attribute to the white man, made the Ho-Chunk vulnerable. The Illinewek and Fox encroached on Ho-Chunk territory and war broke out. With fewer numbers, the Ho-Chunk had to flee. Stone Axe told François that was the reason the Ho-Chunk were settling in this less desirable territory. It was less contested."

14 Août 1712
"They were finally traveling back north and camped again where the rivers join. That's the point where they last saw the de L'Isle's group."

20 Août 1712
"They spotted a small Fox encampment. Father Charles wanted to stop. Stone Axe agreed and said it would have been an insult to pass by. They were welcomed but were all concerned because they didn't know if these Fox knew of the massacre at Grosse Pointe or of the siege of their tribe at Butte des Morts. While the French weren't directly involved in either attack, they were complicit. Father Charles asked the Fox chief why they are so far west. The answer was vague. Jean told François he thinks they are trying to convince the Sioux tribes to assist them in breaking the siege of Butte des Morts and then help them take more territory from the Ho-Chunk."

25 Août 1712
"Jean insisted that they leave. Father Charles resisted, saying that is what he was there for. Jean made it clear that he didn't think we were safe. Father relented. They left and followed the river west-northwest."

28 Août 1712
"Jean thinks there's still a week of steady paddling to Fort Sainte Antoine and their rendezvous. François says he's getting excited as they near their destination and his setting off to seek his fortune. He's also getting tired of guarding

Father Charles and paddling him around while he attempts to convert the Indians."

8 Septembre 1712

"The weather must have been miserable. He wrote that there was windblown rain all day. They chose to stay in camp till the weather cleared. Stone Axe showed them the way to a cave not far inland where they could keep dry. The walls were marked with line drawings and etchings of animals and figures. Stone Axe said he had only heard of that place from the Ojibwa elders and that farther north there were more sacred places of the spirits."

16 Septembre 1712

"They were back on the river at dawn. Trees were turning color. Stone Axe left them while the rest enjoyed a pipe break. He returned in a short time with five fowl. François didn't hear him fire a shot and he asked Stone Axe how he got the fowl. Stone Axe showed him his weapon, a throw. François described it as stones tied to the end of deer hide strips, which were joined together at the other end. Stone Axe showed him how he would stand up quickly at the edge of the marsh, twirl and throw it over the heads of fowl feeding near shore. When the startled flock frantically rose in flight, some were knocked out of the sky by the spiraling stones. François liked the fowl, but preferred the sturgeon."

18 Septembre 1712

"The group stopped to make camp. Stone Axe has not been at ease since they entered the area he called 'the land of the ancient ones.' He pointed out many mounds in the area. He called them sacred and inhabited by the spirits of the first fathers of his people. Some of the mounds were flat, others conical, and some in the shape of animals. The hills and mounds didn't look like anything special to François, but he recognized Stone Axe's reverence. Stone Axe told them that no tribe claimed this sacred place as their own but that all tribes honored the place. Stone Axe said he would not spend the night with them there. Before he left, he said that they would be safe from attack by the Fox while there, but not safe from the spirits if they were perturbed by the intrusion. Stone Axe told them he would rejoin the group at Sainte Antoine. They saw smoke from a campfire to the south, assumed it was a Fox war party, so decided to chance the 'wrath' of the spirits over an attack by the Fox."

19 Septembre 1712

"The next day they saw Fox warriors in four canoes following them and knew the campfire they saw was theirs. Jean was the most concerned. Stone Axe would not return and would not go near the place of the spirits of the dead, the place of the effigy and conical mounds. They were scattered throughout the area on the nearby island bluff and inland. He wanted nothing of staying there and encouraged the group to leave the sacred place too. François said the group was too tired to comply. They would stay one more night. Stone Axe was their guide and paddler, not their protector—that was the fusliers' and François' role, at least until they reached the fort. No one blamed Stone Axe for leaving."

20 Septembre 1712

"As the others broke camp, François set out to gather some nuts that littered the forest floor near their campsite. He intended to join the Father and the others at the canoes. A short time later he crested a ridge some one hundred *troists* from the river and saw several Fox warriors. François could only watch in horror as the savages shot and bludgeoned Jean and La Blanc and desecrated their bodies. The last to die was Father Charles. As he knelt in shallow water clutching the crucifix he wore around his neck, François said he saw one of the Fox approach Father from behind and nearly cleaved his head with a stone club. François remained still and hidden. The Fox first looked after a warrior who was shot in the groin by Jean just before Jean was struck with an axe. The wounded warrior was laid on the shore of the river. The rest spread out along the shore, apparently looking for François' trail.

"Finding something to eat was important to François because their provisions had run out and they didn't dare shoot a deer or elk for fear that there were more Fox in the area. François had filled his shirt with large green nuts littering the forest floor on a steep bluff, but emptied most of them out after he saw the carnage. He slid back down the hill a short distance, turned and ran north, then back to the trail along the river. He figured he was a few leagues south of where Jean said they would find Fort Sainte Antoine.

"Dad, he says the nuts were green, but I'm sure he was talking about black walnuts and why I had visions and the perception of their taste and smell. There was another wood smell that was recurring too, but I haven't figured that one out."

"You're right about black walnuts, Willa. When they form and ripen, they're green and don't turn black until they fall off the trees in October and lay on the ground for a week or so. In September they would still be green."

21 septembre 1712

"François waded, then swam a short span and took refuge on the bluff we just left. Stone Axe pointed it out before he left the day before and said it was a sacred place, too.

"François speculated that's the reason the Fox didn't attack them in their camp and why they would hopefully avoid coming after him on the bluff. He decided to leave the journal and his possessions except for his musket, ball, and powder. He could see the Fox patrolling the riverbanks, but always keeping a distance from the bluff. He was going to try to leave as little of a trail as possible by wading through the marsh to shore. From there he would try to find a line of four mounds aligned west to east. That was near where the Fox butchered Father Charles, LaBlanc, and Jean, and according to Stone Axe those mounds point toward another sacred area to the east. François said he figured that if the Fox stayed clear of the sacred places, then traveling through them might provide some protection as he tried to escape. It would be a roundabout route, but he thought it was his best chance. Father Charles had made sketch maps of the rivers and François wanted to retrieve them from his body before joining L'Isle. If François reached the fort and L'Isle's party wasn't there, he planned to travel north from the sacred area to the east and try to find a party of trappers or Ojibwas. He vowed to do all he could to muster enough men to dispatch the Fox and give his friends a proper Christian burial. He's worried, though, because it looked like the Fox split into two groups, which would make it more difficult to elude them.

"His last entry is, 'I leave this journal now, and will retrieve it and my satchel when I come back with L'Isle or Ojibwas, lest I am come upon and butchered by the Fox savages.'

"Dad, do you know of any mounds in this area?"

"Only that there are still some around here. Most have been plowed under by farmers or destroyed when roads were built. There should be a record of them of some sort. Why?"

"He said he was going to return to the place where the 'four mounds aligned east and west.' If I can find those mounds at least I will know what direction he was headed when he abandoned the journal. Other than that, I don't know where else to look."

"There is a lot of territory east of here. Even if you find where he was headed, how does that help you?"

"I'm not sure. But he did say that he was headed toward a second area of mounds to the east to take refuge before going to the fort, which is at Perrot Park. Since he didn't come back for his journal, he probably didn't meet up with the other group, or elude the Fox. If he did, I can't believe he wouldn't have retrieved this. At least I have an idea of where to begin looking. Like you said, I need to 'suck it up and find the best option.' Finding this guy might be the only way to resolve this."

"I hope you're right, for your sake. But don't get your hopes up too high. You know, Willa, there's something that might help you—aerial survey maps. The government did surveys in the 1940s of the entire state. Your Uncle Michael and I use them as a resource whenever we're looking to buy a piece of land. Those maps have incredible detail with elevation lines. If there are four mounds aligned east and west and still intact, I'll bet they'd appear on an aerial picture of the area around Trempealeau. Anyway, it's just a thought."

"Thanks, that's a great idea. You're right about not getting my hopes up. But finding his journal—what are the odds? This journal may be the key. At the very least it provides a dose of reality. We found a real thing, related directly to my dreams. For the first time since this all started, I have something tangible and it proves that it can't all just be in my head."

About a mile from home, Dad said, "Until you found that journal, you had me more than a little concerned about your ... well, your obsession and dreams. It all sounded too farfetched to be real. I'm probably as relieved as you are that you found it. So now what do you do? Keep looking for more?"

"What do you mean?" I asked.

"Well, you said you knew most of what was in the journal from your dreams. So the journal confirms that your dreams have a basis in fact. That you couldn't have known these details from any other source. That whatever happened was real and not delusional. Do you really need to find this guy or is this the sum point of this whole experience?"

"No. I can feel it. I need to find him."

"Him. You mean François?" Dad asked.

"Yeah. I don't think the purpose of me hearing the voices, the visions, memories, and smells was to find the journal. I think I was led to the journal so it would help me find him."

"There wasn't anything you read in the journal that says

where he was going except a scant reference to the mounds. How are you going to find him?"

"He said he was going to try to follow the direction of the four mounds to another area of mounds to the east, then head north overland. So, I'll start with your idea and use the aerial maps to look for the mounds on the east side of the bluff.

"That's a lot of country, honey. Do you have any other leads?"

"I think he was buried alive. That's a recurring dream. Maybe a cave-in or as torture or punishment by captors."

"Now you're scaring me again, Willa. How the hell do you expect to find a guy maybe buried somewhere near the Mississippi River 250 years ago?"

"That's the $64,000 question, Dad. There have to be more clues. How the hell could I have found his journal buried 250 years ago? But I did. So why not look for the guy who wrote it?"

"I'm not trying to discourage you, only remind you of how daunting your search is likely to be. Are you ready to spend God only knows how long doing this? Give up on your degree? Or finding a job to start paying back your old man for all those school loans?"

"I don't have a choice. I know continuing with this search sounds obsessive compulsive, it probably is. But if I don't do this, I will go completely crazy. I have to put an end to the nightmares. And Dad, don't worry about the loans, I'm good for it."

"That's not where I was going. I just want to suggest that you keep the big picture in mind during all of this."

"I appreciate that, Dad. I will. But, I have no 'big picture' if I can't put an end to this nightmare. This has at least given me hope."

We arrived back at home. I thanked Dad again for taking me to the bluff and for suggesting the aerial survey maps, but most of all I thanked him for having faith in me.

I was so excited to show this to Dan! After I helped Dad

unhook the "yot" I ran in the house, got my bag, hugged Mom, and said goodbye. I knew Dad would fill her in on our discovery and hopefully leave out the part about the crazy, depressed daughter.

14

I didn't get to Dan's apartment till 1:30 in the morning. He was already asleep. He woke when he heard me. I kissed him hello and told him I found something important and that I couldn't wait to show him. He asked if it could wait till tomorrow. He had an 8:00 a.m. class to teach. Reluctantly I agreed and slipped into bed with him. I would show him the journal when he came back for lunch after class.

Dan wasn't much of a lover. Goes through the motions, but he's just not into it. At first I thought it was me. But I am sensing the same lack of passion for his work, hell for life. Until I get my PhD I can only be an amateur psychologist, but the more I think about what my dad said, it seems he hit the nail on the head. Dan doesn't have confidence in himself. Doesn't trust his own thoughts or views. He has always succeeded, not based on what he thinks, but on what he remembers. And he remembers everything. He trusts that he already has the correct answer or feeling or perspective somewhere in his database. All he has to do is retrieve it, no thinking required.

I've recently gotten past the infatuation and am into the objective evaluation stage of our relationship. And I hate to admit this, but I see Dan in sort of the same way Dad did after talking with him for an hour. I just couldn't put my finger on it before. For something to be believable to Dan he has to have read about it before. But if there is new information or empirical evidence contrary to what he read, he dismisses it.

He did that when looking at the French colonization statement he read in Mackinac, his view of my experiences during the experiment, when I was clubbed by the police on State Street, even buying into that anemic defense of Freud I gave. That is probably how he came across to my dad.

Perhaps Dad and I are underestimating Dan. At least he can read the journal for himself, which is the very sort of information that he finds most credible.

15

The next morning while I waited for Dan to get back to his apartment, I decided to walk the eight blocks to the historical society to do some additional research. I knew Dan would need corroborating evidence and I wanted to be ready. One and a half hours of poring over early Wisconsin history books and maps yielded little, until I saw a name on an old map I remembered from the journal. The mapmaker L'Isle. He was in the other group in François' expedition, and the one who François was trying to meet up with. The date on the L'Isle map in the textbook was 1718. We had seen that map before, but then it only had peripheral relevance. Now I realize that it corroborates the journal entry, coincides generally with the timeline, and means that L'Isle survived and completed his task of exploring and mapping the western territory.

The historical society archivist told me they didn't have aerial survey maps there, but that the campus library probably had a set. She was right, they did. I scoured the map that included the area around Trempealeau. The detailed elevation lines on the maps were just like Dad described. There were lots and lots of hills but none of them looked like conical mounds. Nothing jumped out at me. Mostly out of exasperation I asked the reference librarian for any books on Wisconsin Indian mounds. She returned with a book and said, "Sorry, this is the only one I could find." The title looked promising, *Upper Mississippi—Historical Sketches of* the Mound Builders, the Indian Tribes and Progress of Civilization in the Northwest_by George Gale. But the Northwest was not where I was looking. Then I realized after looking at the publication date of 1845 that Wisconsin *was* America's Northwest. I started reading. Turns out that Judge George Gale owned a couple thousand acres smack dab in the middle of the aerial survey map. And sure enough there were Indian mounds on his land. I started out by looking at his sketches from the nineteenth century side by side with the aerial survey map. The mounds sketched out by Gale didn't appear on the aerial survey. Shoot. They must have all been destroyed or obscured by vegetation and erosion. But just south of Perrot Park was a large effigy mound, maybe a bear. It was on both maps. Immediately to the south of that mound were five conical mounds. Four of them lined in nearly a perfect east and west line. Follow that line east and there is Gales land. The four mounds laid out east and west pointed right to a second area of mounds to the east! I found it! That's probably where François was heading after his last journal entry. What's there now? Galesville, Wisconsin. That's where I resume my search.

I was ready for Dan.

16

Over grilled cheese sandwiches, I showed the journal to Dan. He listened patiently while I read some of the most poignant passages to him. I couldn't tell what he was thinking. He didn't ask any questions or interrupt with a quote from some obscure source, nothing.

When I finished, I said, "Isn't that incredible?"

"It is. You know it's illegal to knowingly disturb a historic site. You were on public land, too, weren't you?"

"That's what my dad said. But there is no way in hell I'm going to leave this find to archeologists and only get a chance to look at it once in a while through a glass case. Even you thought I was crazy. This is critical to establishing the basis of my dreams. So many of the visions I described that occurred in the tank were detailed in that journal, even 'one king, one law, one faith' was in there. Don't you appreciate the significance of this?"

"Of course I do. That's why the archeological evidence needs to be handled by professionals. And I never said you were crazy. I said you were delusional."

"Now what do you think?" I asked.

"I am very happy for you and this find is extraordinary, but your conclusion as to what this means and how it relates to your dreams is conjecture."

"What about the wound I envisioned, and L'Isle, and all the other people and events that align with the journal? That's not conjecture. L'Isle, he's in the journal, published a map and is documented in textbooks that I can show you," I said.

"I understand. But Willa, you really don't know any more now than you did before about the most important issues, the source of your dreams and visions ... your delusions."

"So even finding this journal, which by any measure 'was despite extraordinary odds to the contrary,' I am still delusional if I continue on my little quest? Is that your learned opinion?"

"The overwhelming evidence is that neither you nor anyone else today is able to speak with or share thoughts with someone from 1712. There is no scientific basis for this. Since that is the overwhelming evidence, then belief in the contrary is delusional, yes," Dan answered.

"I have just handed you an incredible trove of evidence. There is no scientific methodology that would explain how the hell I could just walk up a hill and find the very journal recording the very dreams I am having. I was instantly able to speak and read French and I'm an expert in eighteenth-century French history in America. I find four linear Indian mounds pointing to another cluster of mounds just as the journal said I would. So what is your explanation for that?"

"Willa, I don't have an explanation. But the prevailing opinion on symptoms like yours is that you are unconsciously attributing similarities but ignoring differences between your dreams and the ramblings in the journal. You are also translating the content, which can include biased interpretation. These are significant flaws. This is simply not scientifically convincing evidence."

"At what point do my delusions transition into becoming the overwhelming evidence?"

"That's rhetorical."

"Rhetorical! I think defining the answer to that question is critical to finding the answer to this whole thing. Is there any evidence that I could produce that would influence you to think otherwise?"

"That's rhetorical too! There is no way I can give a logical answer to that."

"Okay. So what do you recommend, Doctor?"

"Frankly, I've given it a lot of thought. Richard, Digman, and Horner (1960) and Rickard and Dinoff (1962) used behavior modification to decrease delusional verbal behavior using social stimuli and reinforcement. But their approach really isn't applicable to your symptoms. Instead, the treatment of choice for this type of ... challenge, is anti-psychotic pharmaceuticals. You know I can't prescribe drugs, but I'm sure that I can get a colleague over at the medical college to get you something."

"You've got to be kiddin' me. You spent what, eight years, no, for you that was four or five, studying psychology and psychotherapies and your 'treatment of choice' is to drug me up? Psychology isn't a science, it's a pharmacy according to you! You want a doped-up girlfriend?"

"No. I want a delusion-free girlfriend. And the literature indicates that the right combination of drugs might help. Searching for artifacts is only fueling your delusions, not mitigating them. That isn't a treatment or even progress, it's acting out a fantasy."

"No matter what I do or find isn't going to change your position on this, is it? Dan, I am going to continue my search, period. You know, I didn't hear you answer one of my questions directly. I was either being rhetorical or you told me what some other researcher said. What pisses me off is that by your own admission there is no documented case with comparable characteristics to mine. So instead of thinking about this as a unique situation, you insist on trying to plug in some bullshit you read once, and somehow you think doing that is helpful. To me, you are disbelieving something despite overwhelming evidence to the contrary that I just proved to you. And how you can find that that is not delusional in *your* case, but is in my situation, is beyond me," I said.

"Look Willa, I'm trying to balance my responsibility as a

psychologist and my personal concern for someone I care about. I gave you my opinion as a psychologist that there is a treatment option. As your professor your input from the experiment is an aberration and shouldn't be considered. That undermines the reliability of the data and I won't be able to publish it. As your boyfriend I want to be supportive. I want it to be like it was before all this started. So, as your boyfriend, if you'd like me to come with you on your next excursion, I will."

I think he was trying to be funny when he added, "... and I can help ensure that you don't damage any more archeological sites."

Was he patronizing me? I was too angry with him to be objective. It seems like this is all about him. I'm embarrassing him, I'm ruining his precious published paper, I'm irrational, needy, and asking for his help. But perhaps I'm the one being selfish here. As I left, I told him I'd think about his offer to come with me, knowing we couldn't go until after the end of the semester.

I took the time to catch up on my assigned reading, finish my final paper, and consolidate my data. I had been struggling with regular episodes of depression, primarily lethargy. Up to this point I had been experiencing with increasing frequency and duration episodes where it was hard to get up in the morning, harder still to read, study, and concentrate. Finding the journal gave me renewed energy and my mood turned manic and kicked in like an adrenaline rush. I was able to get a lot done. Against my better judgment, I left most of my xenoglossy input out of the final paper. I felt guilty about doing that, like I was caving in, wussing out. I didn't report what really was happening because Dan didn't want to see it. I had enough to worry about, so taking the "course of least resistance" in my class work and with Dan seemed best at this point. I turned in my homogenized paper on the last day of class.

17

Before I took Dan up on his offer to come with me on my next "excursion," I wanted to be as sure as I could that it would be worthwhile, recognizing that this whole thing was the proverbial "needle in a haystack" endeavor. In spite of that, I had already found one needle and that encouraged me to press on. The searching was as exasperating as Dan's resistance, but I was desperate and encouraged by finding the journal.

I had a recurring nightmare of being chased across a small river and up a wooded hill. The shadows cast by the trees indicated the sun was nearly in the middle of the sky to my right. If that is François, that would have meant that around noon he was traveling due east. If he left the bluff just before dawn, headed southeast to the four mounds and then due east, how far would he have gotten by noon? Guessing two or three miles an hour because even though he would likely have been hurrying through the woods to escape, I know from working with my dad in the woods how hard it is to sustain a faster pace. You have to step over windfalls, circumvent blackberry brambles and bogs, cross streams—it's difficult. I figured he made it between twelve and fifteen miles tops. I went to my Gazetter map of Trempealeau County and looked for topography similar to what I remember from the dream of crossing a small stream and steep hill twelve to fifteen miles from the park. It pointed back at Galesville, with my best guess being an area just northeast of town. I knew who I was looking for. I had an idea of where to look. But I still had no idea of what I was looking for. Maybe another stash of evidence, his grave or another clue of some sort. I decided that just like the bluff, if I saw it I would recognize it, and the only way that would happen is if I go there and snoop around.

With Dan's full schedule we didn't have a free weekend until June 18th. Dan said he'd accompany me if I could wait till then. I decided to wait and invite him along just in case I found something. At least then Dan would see one more piece of evidence that this was real and not delusional. If we found nothing, I was no worse off. He thinks I'm crazy anyway.

We left at eight o'clock Saturday morning. It was unseasonably cool, but the clear blue sky with the full moon still visible overhead gave me a feeling that this would be a good day. Since we would be in the area and Dan had friends in La Crosse he wanted to visit, we decided to drive separately. He planned to help me poke around for the day. I would either stay the night in Galesville or drive home alone.

Dan followed me. When we arrived in Galesville, we parked near a diner. Dan got into my car and together we drove through town and the surrounding countryside.

"What are you looking for," Dan asked me for the third time since we arrived.

"I really don't know for sure. But I'll know when I see it. Just like when I saw the bluff."

We circled back to the diner for lunch. It was bright inside, with a combination of overhead fluorescent lights, south-facing floor-to-ceiling windows, and white and black tiles on the walls and counter. There were six red vinyl stools, the stainless steel pedestals bolted to the floor. Two men occupying stools stopped sipping their coffee long enough to turn in unison to eye up the new customers. There were five booths on the periphery. The only booth not along the windows was already occupied. Dan motioned toward the next closest booth and we sat down. The top of the table was still damp from being bused and wiped off after the previous customer left. When I say wiped off, I mean a damp cloth was run over maybe a third of the table. Based on the number of crusted and sticky spots I found simply by placing my arm on the table that it probably had not been thoroughly cleaned since the place opened. The menu was slightly less sanitary. I wished I had a sponge and Clorox. But I was famished and when the waitress came by, I ordered the house special—the cheeseburger basket. Dan wrinkled his nose at my choice and ordered a salad. He's been on a diet for the last couple of months and acts like because he is, I should be too. No way. Especially now, when I'm in action mode and focused, I'm hungry.

"We could probably both stand to lose a couple of pounds," he said.

You jerk. You're the one with the belly starting to spread open the bottom buttons of your shirt and are on the last notch of your belt. With all the stress recently and not feeling like eating during my depressions, even the insatiable appetite I get during manic periods like this hasn't compensated. I've lost two dress sizes since February, down to a size four, and we "both could lose a couple of pounds!"

"So, we're here. Now what? We've driven up and down every street in this town and what have you learned?" he said.

"Dan, I told you a dozen times, I will know it when I see it. We just need to be patient."

"Patient! Willa, I have tried to be patient. I have listened to every one of your dreams about your French pal, about being chased around the woods, buried alive. And here we are driving around some 'burg' looking for 250-year-old clues. It is really hard to be patient!"

The waitress returned with our food. I dug in. Dan talked. He asked me how could I still think this quest was rational. He didn't wait for an answer, I was still chewing. When he finished another brief diatribe, I swallowed my mouthful of fries and tried to answer. Since we had this discussion multiple times before, I tried to stick to key points that I felt were compelling: finding the mountain in the river and the journal, and the historical veracity of the memories and visions. He either cut me off or gave a preconceived rebuttal to each statement.

I see that taking Dan on this trip was a mistake. "Dan, I appreciate you coming with me, but if that is how you feel about this you should probably leave. Go to La Crosse, I'll be fine."

"You know, I think I will. This is just too crazy for me."

He set his fork in his unfinished salad and left before I could get up to give him a hug.

He was right to be frustrated. Hell, I was frustrated. I'm compelled to find a resolution and Dan is repelled by what he views as the futility of the whole thing. And so far, this was just another time-consuming and futile dead end, just like Dan said.

"I have those dreams, too," blurted someone behind me.

I turned around to see who spoke. Sitting alone in the only other occupied booth was a disheveled hippie, probably late twenties—hard to tell. I barely noticed him sitting there when we came in. He got up, walked across the diner, and plopped himself down where Dan had been sitting.

He was tall, gangly, and hairy—his unattended beard a mix of brown, red, and blond. Piercing blue eyes peeked from under the visor of a faded and stained Green Bay Packer "AFL-NFL World Champions" cap that failed to restrain a disheveled mop of hair. He had a tie-dyed T-shirt under an unzipped gray hooded sweatshirt. Unzipped I see, because the pull was missing. It was adorned with an array of spots and stains. He had a peace sign fashioned from heavy gauge copper wire, held around his neck with what looked like a leather shoestring. His knee peeked through a thin circle mesh of threads on his worn bell bottom jeans. His fingernails and cuticles were stained with a variety of colors. It looked like he had put on a different primary color of nail polish on each digit and only partially removed it. He would have looked right at home on campus in Madison.

114

He also brought with him an odd aroma. Best I could tell it was a combination of turpentine, B.O., and weed.

"Who's the douche bag?" he asked.

"That *douche bag* is Doctor Janis, a psychology professor at Wisconsin."

"He's still a douche."

Geez, I'm getting hit on by a Galesville townie.

Maybe not. He seemed to get dead serious and straight to the point. "I've had the nightmares for almost two years. They started just before I moved here from Edina. I must have tripped on some bad acid. Can't get that French asshole out of my head."

"What makes you think he's French?" I asked, wondering if he had just overheard something I told Dan.

"Sometimes I see a word or two written and hear voices speaking in French. I assumed the guy was French," he answered.

Before I got too excited I wanted to be sure he just didn't repeat to me what he overheard from my conversation with Dan. "You live here?" I asked.

"Yeah. Bought a small farm east of town with my chick and a couple of dudes. We were going to live off the land. It'd be cool. We grew our own food, had a few chickens, ducks, big garden. Grew our own pot, too. Then it got bogus. Frenchie came into the picture. Fucked with everybody's mind, but mostly mine. I swear that farm is haunted. One by one everybody left, but me. It was too heavy, they just couldn't take it anymore."

"Take what exactly?"

"For me it was mostly the nightmares. But everyone could feel a presence and cold chill when you'd walk out of the house. It'll be eighty outside, you walk onto the porch and a 'wooosh' of freezing air hits you. Voices too. In French, 'Help me, get me out of here,' praying, that kind of bullshit. Like I said, fucks with your mind after a while. I used to paint. People said my stuff was pretty good, very 'DeKooning.' Now when I try to paint it comes out Baroque for God's sake. It's not my stuff. It's the nightmares. I gotta take a leak."

With that he left.

The waitress, with *Claire* sewn on her pink and white striped blouse, came to the table with a pot of coffee. She looked toward the restroom and rolled her eyes. "You want a refill, Hon?"

"Sure." I couldn't take my eyes off the long ash precariously hanging from the cigarette in her mouth. "Does he live around here?" I wanted to double check his story.

"Yup. He's got a small farm off County Trunk B. A little odd sometimes, but he's harmless."

Claire returned to her spot behind the counter.

The restroom door squeaked and banged opened, then slammed shut behind my table guest as he made his way back.

"I'm Willa by the way," I said as he sat.

"Ken, Ken Ludwig. So do you think I'm pretty fucked up?"

"That wouldn't be my description, no." He looked at me as though he was fully expecting a more vigorous defamation. "I don't think you're fucked up at all. Unless I am, too. I hear 'Frenchie' regularly, have the nightmares, the visions, the cries for help, and the praying. In fact that's why I'm here."

Ken looked at me with a combination of relief and excitement. "What the fuck, I thought the sonofabitch was just haunting my farm. Probably isn't my guy though. My French guy died over two hundred years ago. Was buried alive and has been pissed off ever since," Ken said.

He shared things that Dan and I didn't talk about at all. Ken may actually be channeling François, too! I pulled the journal out of my bag and slid it across the table toward him. He started to reach for it but stopped. "Go ahead, open it," I said.

He carefully lifted the fragile cover and started to read the French writing without hesitation, just as I had the first time I saw it. His voice expressing disbelief, whispered, "Where did you get this?"

"About fifteen miles from here. There were clues in the nightmares. The visions were so clear that I just needed to find the right spot."

"You're shittin' me!"

"No, I'm pretty sure I'm not. He's been in my head, too. I can't study, people think I'm crazy, and it's ruining my relationship with my boyfriend."

"The douche bag?" he asked.

"Yeah, the douche bag," I answered.

"No big loss."

"It is to me. Anyway, I've got to see your place. There has to be something that drew me here," I said.

"Whoa. Nobody comes to my place. Ever. I'm not letting some pushy broad invite herself over, Frenchie or not."

"Pushy broad! You listen to me, you plopped yourself down here. We're in this together whether either of us likes it or not. I'm not gallivanting up and down this state for seven months to let some townie-hippie tell me I can't look on his goddamn farm when I'm this close to finding out what the fuck has been happening! Now just suck it up and let's do this!" Oh, God, I sound like my dad.

More amused than anything, Ken said, "Noooo ... that's no pushy broad."

I had to laugh, too. He had a point. When I'm in one of my energized, focused, manic states, watch out.

"Okay," I said, trying to calm myself down before starting again. "Look, I respect your privacy, but each of us has unanswered questions, missing pieces in our nightmares. If we can collectively put our visions together, maybe we can figure this out. I will not accept that this is going to persist for the rest of my life. I don't want to spend my life this way. Do you want to end up thirty years from now the hermit artist in the haunted farm at the end of the road?"

"I don't do company. My place is a mess. My head hasn't

been on straight for two years. This is pretty damn hard for me to get my brain around."

"Don't worry, I won't be looking to award any 'Good Housekeeping' seals of approval. But I want to see if your visions, the ones you paint, are the same as mine. Are we haunted by the same thing? Aren't you curious, too?"

"I am. But this is just too weird."

"Here, Ken," I said, pushing the journal back in front of him. I opened it to the last entry. "Read this page."

He read the entire entry, looked up slowly and said, "That's my guy. I've seen that cliff in my dreams. I painted that cliff. I thought that might have been where he fell or jumped from. Okay, you can look around outside my place a little."

"I've got to see the paintings of your visions, too."

"Oh shit, you're just not going to take no for an answer, are you?"

"Not when I'm this close!" I said.

"All right, but make it short and sweet. Follow me. I'll pull my truck around front," Ken sighed.

18

I started to second guess my decision to follow this guy back to his farm. Claire did say he was harmless, she saw us leave, and it was broad daylight. But I still wished Dan had stuck around for this, the douche bag. I laughed to myself.

After a short drive the battered blue pickup I was following pulled into a gravel driveway. An electric company truck was a couple hundred yards down the road. Looked like the crew was trimming tree limbs from above the electric wires. That was reassuring.

Ken hopped out of his truck. I parked right behind him and stepped out. I instantly felt a chill.

"Come over here and stand for a minute," Ken called.

I complied and walked up the wooden steps and stood next to him on his porch.

At first I thought I heard someone hum, but it was more a murmuring din. The murmur grew progressively louder, until it drowned out all other sounds.

"Did you hear that?" Ken asked.

"Of course I heard that. It was deafening."

"It can get even worse. Come around to the back of the house," Ken motioned with his arm.

Thigh-high grass and goldenrod grew between the house and the barn. A narrow path worn by Ken's frequent trips cut through the weeds on a direct line to the barn door. "Now what do you hear?" Ken asked.

I paused and listened. "Nothing. Well nothing out of the ordinary."

"That's what I thought. I rarely hear anything anywhere

except in the front yard or the porch," Ken said matter-of-factly.

"Can I see your paintings now?"

"I hoped you wouldn't need to after hearing the roar on the porch. That's where most people get freaked out and leave," he said.

"After what I've been through Ken, it's going to take more than some murmuring to freak me out. Let's see what you've got inside."

Ken walked me to the back door to the summer kitchen of the old farmhouse. Stepping inside, he led the way along a path winding through the maze of trash piled on and around a huge green and white porcelain wood-burning cook stove, old farm tools, and new and used canvases on and next to an easel perched in the sunniest corner.

"What about those pictures," I asked, gesturing toward the easel.

"They're shit," Ken said.

The inside of the house was slightly less cluttered than the summer kitchen. Every wall seemed to be part of the same mosaic made up of countless paintings.

"Are these all your work?" I asked.

"Sure are. Oh, except that one," Ken said, pointing to an obviously incongruous picture of a tri-masted schooner on a choppy teal green sea. "It was hanging there when we bought the place, otherwise it's my stuff," he added.

In what might have been a dining room was a striking portrait of a beautiful young woman with her hair piled and propped high on her head.

"That's Shiree," I said.

Ken looked at me with a piercing stare. "How could you possibly know that? I named it 'Cherie.'"

"She was in a dream, with that same look, the same *fontage* and all. Shiree was a name written in the journal you saw."

"Okay. I wasn't sure if your visions and mine were

coincidence or what. But geez, you've seen an awful lot of what I have, too. You're making a believer out of me, Willa."

Ken continued the tour of his work. He paused in front of the several paintings of the island and ledge. They were generally accurate, but I pointed out that the bluffs he painted had too few trees and vegetation, and one of them depicted boulders on the ledges and not the flat limestone strata I saw.

"Everybody's a fuckin' critic," he muttered, I think in jest.

I realized my comments were inappropriate and said, "I'm sorry. I didn't mean to be rude. The pictures are really quite stunning. It's just that I'm sure your vision is of the same 'Mountain in the River' where I found the journal. I was there. I saw the bluff, that's all I meant."

"Don't worry about it. I'm way past being sensitive about my work. If I like it, I don't give a rat's ass what anybody else thinks," he said.

"Do you like these?"

"Fuck no. I painted most of them just to get the images out of my head. Usually doesn't work though, they're either replaced by another or a rerun of a previous one. It's like when I was actually painting pictures and would get an inspiration. I'd be painting and suddenly it would just flow. I couldn't paint fast enough. The image, colors, brush strokes just came. I didn't have to think about it. Would completely lose track of time, sometimes painting all night. That was fun and what I loved about the medium. Now when I get in one of those frenetic mindsets, it isn't due to inspiration, but an involuntary, inexplicable, compulsion to paint an image in my head whether it's from a dream or just psycho. I feel like the only way I can get that image out of my head is to get it on canvas."

I was fascinated, actually comforted, by Ken's description of his state of mind. In a lot of ways that is how I felt, too. While listening to Ken I looked at the pictures, empathizing with him. On the wall of the stairway going to the second floor was a series of paintings of deeply contorted faces surrounded by darkness.

"That's Frenchie, I think," Ken said, noticing where I was looking. "If he didn't drown in the river, he must have been buried alive. Anyway, that's what I think he's trying to tell me, so that's what I am compelled to paint."

"Ken, you've captured in paint exactly what I've been seeing in my dreams, too."

"Except for the elevations, boulders and shadows, I guess," he reminded me.

"I had that coming. It's eerie to look at real pictures of my delusions," I said.

"Okay. So we both know Frenchie. What the fuck can we do about?"

I suggested that we meet back at the diner tomorrow morning at 8:00. Ken would bring any notes or sketches he had and I'd bring my notes from my lab work and the journal. We would try to piece together what we had and try to figure out what his front yard has to do with this.

"The sonofabitch is buried on my farm. We can compare notes, talk and talk all we want, but until we dig him up and book him back to Parie or wherever the hell he needs to be, we're screwed."

"You might be right. I'll call my dad tonight. He has a backhoe. Hopefully, we can get him to come down here. If not, I don't know what I'll do. Maybe as a last resort I can convince an archeological team at the university to do some digging, but I would probably need Dan to put in a good word for me, and I don't think that would happen."

"Your dad doesn't think you're completely bonkers? My family wants nothing to do with me. Hell, they were sure I was nuts years before Frenchie paid a visit."

"Dad might have thought that when I first talked to him. But he was with me when we found the journal. He knows there's something to this besides his daughter being crazy. I'm sure he'd help if he could."

"Cool, but what can he do besides dig up my yard?"

"I don't know. But I want to get his take on this. At least we can get an objective view, maybe he will have some thoughts. I'll call him. Will I see you tomorrow morning at the diner?" I asked.

"Well, I don't have my social calendar with me, but I can probably fit it in," Ken said with a smile.

19

I arrived at the diner at 7:30 the next morning from the Motel 6 that I stayed at in Trempealeau. I needed coffee. Hadn't slept at all the night before.

When I walked in, there was Ken sitting in the same booth he had been in before he joined me the day before.

"Did you spend the night here?"

"Probably should, it's a lot nicer than my place. Take a load off, have a seat. We may need more coffee though. I put a big dent in the first pot," Ken said.

I was happy to see him and quickly slid into the vinyl seat across from him. Something was different about Ken. Did he take a shower this morning? Gone was the aura of turpentine and B.O. Still a hint of weed, and is that ivory soap?

Once I was seated, Ken said, "I couldn't sleep last night. I kept thinking about that journal and you."

Evidently thinking that didn't come out how he meant it, he added, "I mean how strange it is that you have the same crazy visions and dreams I have. It's reassuring to think someone else is just as screwed up as I am."

"I'm happy my torment is a comfort to you," I said dryly.

"You know what I meant," Ken said.

"I know. Say, I talked to my dad last night. He may be able to come down here in a week or two, maybe sooner. He's only about one and a half hours away and I think he is worried about me."

"Well that's fine, but I don't know what you expect he's going to do."

"I'm not sure either. But, he's still worried about me and probably feels that coming here to help is a convenient way to check on me, and frankly his objectivity may be useful."

"So, when did your dreams start anyway, Willa?"

"During my first experience in a sensory deprivation tank. I'm working on my PhD in psychology. That's what my thesis research project is on. A sensory deprivation tank is a ..."

"Yeah, I know what it is," he said. "Before I became a prolific artist and hemp farmer extraordinaire, I was majoring in Ed. Thought I'd make a cool hippie-dippie art teacher. Anyway, it would have been a job. In my child psych class we studied the effects of sensory deprivation on child development. It's heavy shit, and can be a sonofabitch on brain development. I remember those sad pictures of baby monkeys taken from their mothers, clinging desperately to a cloth-covered wire mesh."

"Yeah, that was Harry Harlow's work on surrogate mothers. He's a big deal at Wisconsin. Some of my undergrad work was on his research. But, let's go back. You were going to be an art teacher? I'm not sure the world of education would have been ready for you!"

"Maybe not this crazy asshole, but when I was just a studious crazy artist, maybe then," he chuckled.

"So why aren't you teaching Monet to middle schoolers?"

"First, I hate kids. Second, I had to get off the grid. Lost my student deferment. My draft lottery number is ninety-seven, November 18th birthday. They drafted all the way up to 193 and were shipping every kid who could walk in by themselves off to Fort Dix for basic training, then 'Nam two weeks later. Bummer. No fuckin' way for me. I was not going to fight for nothin' in a goddamn rice paddy halfway across the world. For what? Some corrupt, puppet South Vietnam government. Help Nixon wiggle out of there? Bullshit. Well, the Man seems to take that draft shit pretty seriously.

So when I didn't respond to their letter about losing my student deferment, they came lookin' for me. I got outta Dodge.

"Before I left, a bunch of art school buddies had a party. I got talked into dropping some acid. They said I'd never see colors or abstract the same way again. Figured what the hell. But that was one bad trip. It lasted a couple of days and that was when I started hearing from Frenchie. First visions, nightmares, and voices. Finally, I think he led me right here. Like I told you yesterday, a couple buddies and their chicks decided they wanted to buy a farm and live the 'back to nature' thing. Well I needed to be somewhere I wasn't going to be found so I joined them. My girlfriend thought it was a great idea and came along. They were having trouble finding a place. We were all checking around. I read about this farm when it was listed in a brochure I got from United Farm Agency.

"I knew immediately this was it. I didn't know why, but once I visited with the realtor I wouldn't consider any other place. I was obsessed with buying this farm and talked the others into coming here. It was Frenchie. Just like I have to paint the images that asshole puts in my head. Once we moved in, Frenchie showed up in a big way and fucked everything up. We started growing and smoking weed to cope. For me it was the only thing that gave me any relief from the dreams and visions. I was getting weird, and the place was freaking everyone out. Eventually everyone else left. I couldn't. They'll arrest my ass the first time I show myself. So here I stay, and here you are."

"Where's your girlfriend now?"

"No fuckin' clue. I don't think living on a 'back to nature' farm with a burned-out artist turned out to be everything she had hoped it would be. When the murmuring and the chill on the porch got worse, well that was the last straw."

"Okay, so what do we do about François Renaulti?" I asked.

"I don't think we accomplish anything unless we find him. At least I'll feel better. Maybe we have to drive a stake through his heart. Would it be too much to ask that he died with a couple of million in gold he took from the Spanish?" Ken said.

"I am not counting on finding any gold. Where do we start the search?" I said.

"Well, it seems pretty clear from both of our dreams that he was buried alive. If it's on my farm, then we just need to start digging."

"Where? Do we dig up your front yard? Driveway? Under your house? Unless we're real lucky, we could be digging for years. I think we should mark anywhere we feel a chill or hear murmurs and look for any anomalies in the yard, or trace evidence. Maybe a part of the yard that has settled, or stones piled somewhere that don't belong? Approach it like archeologists might," I said.

"That makes sense, Willa. But, I'm not very optimistic."

"Hi Suzie!" Ken said to the cute, skinny little thing that came to our table.

"Either of you want more coffee?" she asked, looking only at Ken.

"I would," I said, interrupting her flirtations toward Ken.

"How 'bout you, Kenny?" she asked, still without looking at me.

"You bet. Fill it up and keep it comin'."

She poured coffee in Ken's cup then splashed a little in mine.

"Willa, how about something to eat. I'm famished," he said.

"I am too. Breakfast sounds pretty good."

Suzie took Ken's order. I think he ordered everything on the menu. Three eggs over easy, ham, blueberry pancakes, toast, and orange juice. Geez.

Then she looked at me. "What can I get for you ma'am," she said, emphasizing the *ma'am*.

Really, sweetheart? I thought.

"Two scrambled eggs, toast, and orange juice, please," I said, trying to hide my disdain.

"It'll be right up," she said as she left.

I looked back at Ken to see if there was any reaction. None, but I was miffed at that waitress's rudeness.

"What are you thinking about so intently?" Ken asked.

"Nothing. Just how hungry I am, I guess."

We decided it was silly to start digging until we could narrow down the search area.

With the last piece of pancake secured in his mouth, Ken said, "Can you give me directions to that bluff? I've got to see if it's the same bluff. And if there are any boulders on it or not."

"Of course. But it's only fifteen or twenty minutes from here. We could just drive up there."

"We'll see how this goes," Ken said.

I can't believe Ken finished his whole breakfast before I did. He was looking impatient, so I chugged the last of my orange juice. After employing some higher math, we split the bill and got up to leave. I watched Ken look over his shoulder and smile and wave to our waitress. She emphatically waved and smiled back.

I followed Ken back to his farm to begin an organized search for clues that might lead us to François' resting place and maybe an end to this nightmare. I had to get back to Madison tomorrow so just hoped that we could keep the search moving forward.

We decided to start by walking off grids in Ken's front and side yards. We were looking for any anomalies.

By mid-afternoon we finished. Our best hope rested with two depressions within twenty feet of each other that looked promising. Both were rectangular, one was tantalizingly the size of a grave. We decided it was worth digging, but agreed that no archeologist would be interested based on this scant information. I asked Ken if he was okay with me going home and trying to convince my dad to come back with me and bring his backhoe.

"I sure as hell don't want to dig that by hand. Who knows

how deep we will have to go? If your dad will do it, let's let him do it."

"Okay, but I've got to go home, pack up, and get back to Madison tomorrow. Since my dad can't come for a week or two anyway, why don't we reconvene two weeks from today? Does that work for you?"

"Works for me."

20

When I got home I thought it was time to fill my mom in on François before I approached Dad about going to Galesville with me. I try not to tell Mom things that might cause her to worry. She tends to stress out and dwells on them. Dad probably worries, too, but doesn't show it as much, so I tell him first and get his take on things. His input is always objective, Mom's is more emotional. I'm sure she knows something is going on beyond what Dad has probably told her. I want to fill her in and now is as good a time as any.

Mom told me that Dad was delivering an old truck the company sold to a farmer near Medford and wouldn't be back for hours. She seemed happy to have me alone without my dad. I can tell she feels left out of our discussions sometimes and she's right. Some things I can talk to Dad about that I know would just freak out my mom. She'd worry, I'd regret telling her, and try to backtrack with a varnished version. Why stress us both out? But I think it's time she hears from me what I've been going through. She'll find out about it eventually.

We sit on our sun porch each with a cup of tea. "Isn't it beautiful this time of year, everything is so green?" she asked.

I took a moment to see the backyard. I was looking at it, but not seeing it. The deep purple, violet, white, and red flowers were striking against the emerald cedars behind them. The blooms periodically swayed when the visiting hummingbirds and bumblebees came and went from blossom to blossom.

"It is. This is when I miss being up here the most. Madison is nice, but it's just not the same as looking out at the woods and the garden. Your phlox and bee balm are really doing well."

"Thank you, dear. We planted them two years ago. Your dad and I wanted to be sure what we planted would be hardy enough to make it through these winters. What brings you home?"

"Actually, I wanted some time to talk to you alone."

"How nice. I know you had some things you wanted to talk to Dad about."

"It's just that I think you'd worry about it, that's all."

"Well what is it, Willa?"

"I'm having some problems with my psych project."

"Yes, your dad told me you were struggling with some things."

"I am. Not only have I been getting lower grades on my papers but I'm having side-effects from the sensory deprivation experiments."

"What kind of side-effects?" Mom asked.

"Mostly nightmares. At first they occurred just during the experiments. But for months now I have them almost every night and sometimes recurring as visions during the day. I don't sleep well and that's taking a toll on me."

"Do you need sleeping medication? Maybe you should drop out of the program for a while."

"Sleeping pills don't help, Mother. I'm past the drop out date so we have to pay for next semester whether I finish it or not. I may as well suck it up and try my best to get through it."

"Ah, your father's advice for every crisis," Mom said, and we both laughed. "What kind of nightmares do you have?"

"It's hard to describe, but generally I seem to get visions about a man who lived a couple of hundred years ago. I see what he saw, know what he knew. It's really weird."

"Does this have something to do with the trip to that park you took with your father?"

"Yes. That's why we went. It turns out that these visions and thoughts pertain to a person that really lived. I pieced together as much information as I could from the dreams and talked Dad into helping me look for clues. We drove to the Mississippi to a spot Dad thought sounded like what I have envisioned. He was right. I knew it immediately when I saw it. We even found artifacts left there by that man."

"How do you know it was left there by him and not some prankster?" Mom asked.

"It was buried in a spot I felt like I knew and had obviously been there since the 1700s."

"I don't understand how your dreams, that park, that man, and your psych class are related."

"I'm not sure I do either, but they started when I was submerged for several minutes underwater as part of my class. That seemed to trigger the voices and visions. Now they happen all the time, not just during class."

"Do you need to see someone?"

"What do you mean? A psychiatrist?"

"Well yes. This sounds scary. I'm worried about you."

"Maybe that's what I'll end up doing. But for the time being, I want to try to find out what has been going on and resolve it. If I can't find out for myself, I think I might need help."

"Can Dan help you in that area?"

"No. He wants nothing to do with this, except to put me on anti-psychotic drugs. Thinks it will ruin his standing among his colleagues if he's involved with what he feels are just a series of delusions. There is too little scientific research done in this whole area for him to think it's credible." Shit, I can feel the tear glands kicking in. I'm starting to lose it.

Mom sees it immediately and sits next to me on the settee, followed by a long hug.

"Is this why your father didn't think much of Dan?"

133

"No. Dad thinks that Dan relies on his ability to remember, and recites what he's read without really thinking
through the issue and developing his own opinion. I talked
up how smart Dan was to you two, and I guess Dad was just
disappointed that Dan didn't live up to my billing."

"What do *you* think Dan should do?"

"Help and support his girlfriend. If this is just delusions
and a psychotic episode like he thinks, then why are there
artifacts exactly where I see them? There is a journal written in French that I can read easily. French, Mother! I never
took a French class and we're all Germans. How does that
happen if it's just delusional? I even ran into some guy near
that park who has the same visions as I do. Exactly the
same. Dan seems embarrassed about me. He sure as hell
hasn't been supportive. He went with me to Mackinac Island
to help me research, but whined the whole time. Then he got
frustrated and left me in Galesville this week. This is really
coming between us and it hurts. I think I love him and will
likely lose him over this if I can't figure it out."

"He *is* a doctor of psychology, dear."

"Yeah, but he's also a boyfriend. He sure doesn't act like
it, though!"

"What are you going to do next?"

"Like I said, I ran into a guy who has the same visions I
do. He's an artist and paints what he sees. His paintings are
my visions, too. We think our Frenchman is buried on his
farm. I'm going to try to talk Dad into bringing his backhoe
down there and dig in a few spots. If we don't find anything,
I don't know what I'll do. Probably drop out of school and
see a shrink."

"Your father is very busy at the mill, but you know that
we will do what we can to help. Do your brothers know about
this?"

"Yeah. I went to Superior with Mike earlier this summer
and told him some of it. I'm sure he talked to Peter about it."

Suddenly, the phone rang. Mom ran to the kitchen to

answer. "Willa, it's your father. Would you like to talk with him?"

"Yeah, be right there ... Hi, Dad."

"Hi, honey, I wish I was home. But like I just told your mom, I won't be home till tomorrow. I don't want to drive all the way back from Mellon at night. My night vision is going to pot so I've just checked into a motel. What's new with you?"

"Sorry I missed you, too. I was hoping to convince you to come to Galesville with me with a backhoe. Remember I told you about Ken, the guy that has the same visions I do? Well, we found a few depressions in a couple of spots on his farm that look suspiciously like graves."

"This week is out for me, Willa. I just can't get away. But I would be happy to go with you next Saturday."

"It's a date, Dad. It'll be a long couple of weeks for me. I just can't wait to get this over with one way or another."

"I understand. You know, Willa, under different circumstances this would sound like a real wild-goose chase. But after you walked me up that bluff right to those artifacts, I can't wait to see what you've got in store for me this time."

"Thanks for the vote of confidence, Dad. See you soon."

Mom and I talked for another hour before I headed back to Madison. When I got there, Dan called my apartment and asked me to come over for dinner, then go out for drinks later. I was looking forward to seeing him again and was thinking of apologizing for my stubbornness. He even sounded like he may be trying to make amends. I hope so. Maybe he will be more supportive. I'm not looking forward to telling him I'm going back to Galesville to dig for a burial site. I miss the times we had before this damn lab project started.

21

I got to Dan's ten minutes late. He hates it when I'm late. His attitude seems to be that his time is so much more valuable than mine. It probably is, but it would be nice if he stifled that. I was late for a reason today. I wore a new blue miniskirt outfit, new shoes, and put my hair in a French braid. I took a little more time getting ready. I wanted to look nice. Dan likes it when I dress up a little and usually finds a reason to take me out somewhere when I do. I was a lot more comfortable in jeans, and this outfit made me feel more like a hooker than a grad student, but that's just me. I think he was glad to see me and said I looked great. He was a little hard to read though, perfunctory kiss and all.

He was fussing over dinner—small hunk of baked salmon seasoned with lemon pepper, and a spinach and tomato salad. His damn diet. I could have used a loaded baked potato, too, but kept that to myself and gushed over his effort, since "we both need to watch our weight."

Dinner was fine, the conversation strained. He was trying hard to avoid talking about François and that was all I wanted to talk about.

"Let's hit a few bars. We haven't done that for a while," Dan said.

We were on our second beer when Dan turned serious. "I'm really concerned about you, Willa. You're not giving up on these delusions of yours, are you? Your class work has suffered and you barely made it through the second semester with a B-plus, and it has affected our relationship. I just don't feel like I know you anymore."

"Yes, I realize that."

"I know you do. But your persistence has become an obsession. When depression, delusion, and obsessive thoughts begin to affect your normal life, that's the definition of pathological."

"So we haven't gotten past the point where you think I'm psychotic, is that it?"

"Well, that's part of it."

"Don't let me just hang here Dan, what's the rest of it?"

"As a psych professor, your recent conduct and our relationship, is, well, embarrassing."

"I embarrass you?!"

"Your obsession and behavior do, yes. Willa, I have worked hard to get a good reputation at this university. I don't want to throw that all away because my girlfriend has a problem she refuses to deal with," Dan continued.

"Refuses to deal with! Dan, you're such an asshole!"

Oh my gosh. He looks shocked. Those puppy dog eyes. I bet no one has ever called him an asshole before. How did such an asshole get away so long without anyone saying, "Hey, asshole." I wonder if I should share Ken's assessment of him now? You're a douche bag, too. That just might be too much for the professor to handle at one time. I'll keep that under wraps for the time being.

"Dan, the last thing I would ever want is to be an embarrassment to you, undermine your 'stellar' reputation and your career over some silly little dreams I've been having."

"They're not silly little dreams, Willa."

"I was being facetious, Dan. I know where you're heading with this and I think you're right that we should stop seeing each other for a while."

"Well, if you think that is best thing for us, then I guess we should."

"For us? Whose stellar reputation is being sullied by his psychotic girlfriend? Who is being embarrassed here? Oh yeah, I guess that was you, wasn't it, Dan. Don't pretend you're thinking of what is best for anyone but yourself. Look, I get it. Before I say anything I'll regret, I better go," I said.

"Wait, I'll give you a ride home."

"No!" With that I left. Ten steps out the door I realized the shoes I thought were perfect for the outfit were miserable for walking the full length of State Street and four blocks up Park. Before I made it fifty feet, it started to rain ... then pour. I cried all the way home and decided to burn the outfit and shoes as soon as I got there.

Over the last beer in my fridge, I reviewed the events of the last few months in my mind. What the hell did I just do? This is a guy I really cared about. I introduced him to my parents. My professor. The man who holds the future of my education in his hands. And I call him an asshole. What's worse is that after summer break I'll be starting my second year of the PhD program and I don't know if that's what I want to do, or if my grades from last semester will be good enough to let me graduate. But none of that matters if I can't get rid of these haunting visions and nightmares. What if Dan is a professor for one of my classes? Without a PhD though, it's worthless trying to find a job in the field of psychology. But if I leave the program, I still have eight months on the lease of my outrageously expensive hole of an apartment that I rented so I could live near campus. This is the first summer I haven't worked full time and I owe my parents a ton of money. Do I go deeper in debt and finish the program? Even if I finish the class work, I may not be awarded a PhD because of that B+ I got last semester, and oh yeah, I called my professor and review committee chairman an asshole.

I couldn't sleep at all that night. The next morning I just laid in bed, staying in a fetal position with blankets pulled over my head. I was too lethargic, too hopeless to move. It was my worst episode of depression since this all started. I wasn't sad or angry, just in a dark place emotionally, unable to muster the energy or motivation to do anything. After what seemed like several hours, my thoughts circled around to Ken and the farm. What would his reaction be at hearing that I called Dan an asshole? I couldn't help but laugh to myself, guessing at what Ken would say. That moved me out of the depression just enough and I was able to muster the energy to get on with life again. It was disconcerting though, to think that the states of depression I was experiencing were increasing in intensity and duration. At some point, I may not be able to find a way of snapping myself out of it.

22

Two days later I called Dad. He was home from Mellon and I wanted to tell him all the details about the possible gravesites on Ken's farm that he would help us excavate.

I could tell he wasn't excited about the whole idea, but he reiterated that he'd help.

"Okay, tell me what you want me to do," Dad said.

I explained that we found two depressions similar to the size of a grave, both located on the east side and rear of Ken's farmhouse. One was about eight foot by eight foot and the other four by six.

"How old is this farm?" Dad asked.

"Old. I don't know, at least eighty years old, I guess. Why?"

"Willa, those depressions might just be the remains of the smokehouse and the old outhouse. That's about their size and where they'd be placed. See if you can find any old pictures of the place that show the old homestead as it was back then. If there aren't any buildings where the depressions are, then you might be on to something."

Oh shit. Ken and I hadn't thought of that. I felt completely deflated. Our last best hope was dashed by a dose of reality.

"Willa, are you still there?"

"Yeah. Sorry, I was thinking about what you said and I'm pretty sure you're right. We're too wrapped up in our search for a grave and may have missed the obvious. But it's worth a trip to the library in the area to see if they have any photographs of Ken's farm back in the day."

"Look, I'm happy to help, but none of us has a keen interest in digging up an old latrine. If you find something else let me know. I've got to get to work, but keep me posted."

"Okay, bye Dad."

23

Ken doesn't have a phone. The only way to reach him was either call the diner and hope I catch him, or drive there. I decided to drive.

I went to the barn after knocking loudly on his front door without an answer.

"Are you out here Ken?" I called.

"Yeah, back here."

I found Ken in the back of his barn behind a tarp. He was hanging part of his "crop" up to dry.

"Hi. Looks like it's harvest time?"

"Yup, for these. I start some seeds inside in February under grow lights. They get a good head start. I transplant them outside in the middle of May just after I plant the rest of the seeds out behind the barn. Spreads out the crop a little. I can't harvest the plants that I sowed outside until the end of September. Good crop this year, too. Just look at those flower heads."

"I'll have to rely on your expertise, Ken. Wouldn't know a good marijuana flower if I saw one."

"You'd know if you smoked a little."

"Well, I don't, so I won't."

"Is your dad coming down to dig up Frenchie?"

"Probably not. At least not until we do a little more home-work."

"You couldn't convince him that digging up my front yard was worth the trip?"

"Actually he was happy to do it, but you know what those depressions are?" Without waiting for an answer, "Most likely the old outhouse and smokehouse."

"Oh, fuck. Of course. I hadn't thought of that. Your dad must think we're not only crazy but morons, too."

"I don't think so. But he did suggest we look for old photos of the place. Do you have any?"

"Nope. But I heard one of the old timers at the bar in town call this the old Pederson farm. That might help."

We heard a car door slam. Ken's face went blank and he jogged over to the barn door and peered out, then visibly relaxed.

"Hey man. How's it goin'?"

"Cool. Everything's cool. Just wondered if you had any new weed ready."

"Yeah. Just picked it."

In walked one of Ken's customers. He was about my age, average height, clean shaven, wearing old jeans, t-shirt, wool cap—looked like someone off my dad's logging crew.

"Who's the chick?"

"Just a friend."

"Buyer?" the customer asked.

"Nope, just a friend," Ken said.

"I really liked your last chick."

"Willa, this is Donny. Donny, Willa."

"Nice to meet you," I said.

"Likewise. So how do you know my man?"

"Through a mutual friend," I said. I could see Ken trying to stifle his laugh. Donny saw it too and decided to move on to business.

"I need six ounces."

"Wow. That'll last you for a while, Donny."

"I'm heading to Chicago for a couple of months and don't want to run out. Might sell a little, too."

"Business or pleasure?" Ken asked.

"Both, now that I have some grass."

From out of nowhere, Ken produced a small scale. He

carefully plucked only the small rosettes from four of the inverted six-foot plants. When his hand was full, he put them on the scale and repeated the process a second time.

"Seven and a quarter ounces. How's that? It'll be closer to six once they're completely dry," Ken said.

"The more the merrier, thanks."

Ken took a baggie from a drawer on the workbench and put the weed in. "Donny, you'll need to spread this out on some newspaper for a day or so to make sure it's completely dry before you smoke it."

"Yeah, yeah. How much?"

"How about eighty-five bucks?" Ken said.

"Sounds great."

"Where're you going again, Donny?"

"Chicago."

"Well, have a nice trip," Ken said, as he handed him the bag.

It took me a second to realize that "have a nice trip" was "toker" humor.

"Always do. See you when I get back," Donny called over his shoulder as he left.

Once Donny was out of the barn, Ken laughed, "A mutual friend?"

"Well, in a warped way, more a mutual acquaintance. How do you know Donny?"

"He's the friend of a college buddy. Donny was selling to head shops—bongs, Zig-Zags, that kind of stuff. He's moved on to something legitimate now. He'll probably be a millionaire some day."

"I know it's none of my business, but how many Donnys do you have?" I asked.

"You're right, it's none of your business; about twenty. That's enough to make a living and manageable enough to minimize my risk of being nabbed."

"Got it. So let's start going over the information we have here, go to the library to see if they have any old photographs of your farm. By the way, if you're interested, we could drive up to the bluff so you can see it for yourself," I said.

"Sounds like a plan," Ken said.

We started by carefully pouring over the details from the journal and sharing our collective recollections, memories, and anecdotes on European and North American history between 1690 and 1712 and those specific to François. The visions of the island proved to be both accurate and helpful and we hoped we would find other clues. We knew most of the stuff was irrelevant, but we didn't want to rule anything out as possibly significant and it was interesting to review what we learned about the life of the man that was tormenting both of us.

By piecing together all of the memory fragments, visions, information in the journal, and my history research, Ken and I made the following list of things we think we knew about François.

Black walnuts and basswood trees were significant, as was being buried in a cave, tunnel, or grave, and we were probably close to another significant site.

He was born near the Nive River just outside Bayonne, France, around 1686. His family were farmers, and probably grew peppers and brewed a liquor from it. He loved going to the bull fights and when he was a kid wanted to become a matador. He was recruited by the Regiment de la Marines during the War of Spanish Succession at age eighteen. They waived their height requirement that recruits must be at least five feet five inches so, although too short, François was inducted. He saw action during the siege of Verceil and some other city and was wounded at Oudenaarde. That would have been in 1707. He was discharged in 1708 and returned to Bayonne something of a local hero. That's likely when he met Shiree. Her father was considered aristocratic because of his wealth. He ran a large enterprise that made chocolate, we think. He wanted Shiree to have nothing to do with François. But his own status was tenuous because he was Jewish and the new Edict of Fontainebleau made

Catholic the only acceptable religion in France. Shiree's ancestors fled Spain during the Inquisition and crossed the border into France at Bayonne. Her family was in conflict about whether to move out of France or convert to Catholicism. Shiree was five or six years younger than François.

François was desperate to upgrade his social standing and knew the division of the family farm among him and his four brothers would dilute their individual wealth and status even further.

Two years after he was discharged, the Regiment de la Marines returned to get recruits to go to Fort Royale and Montreal to fight the English in New France. The French had just lost Arcadian and Montreal was in danger. That was the only record of a regiment of French regulars to fight in New France that I could find. François felt lucky to be selected.

He enlisted with the understanding that he would be stationed in Montreal to help build the city's fortifications, but then could be granted an opportunity to claim land for France, trade for furs with the Indians of the western territory and receive a sizeable land grant or an officers' commission for his services. It was on that expedition that he died in 1712. It was clear our visions stopped in the fall of 1712, the last dates in the journal and the likely time of François' death. Before 1690, our memories were dim and faded quickly with each prior year. It seemed we only knew what François knew. We pieced together fragments of information as best we could. François mentioned Bayonne in his journal, and it was likely where he lived because of its proximity to Spain and bull fighting. It was also a port city and the de la Marines primarily recruited in port cities. Bayonne had a sizable Jewish population. The journal referenced his family farm near a river and the Nive, which fits the location as well.

We didn't know if this information would help us find François or not, but we agreed the more we knew the more likely we would find something of value.

We talked more about François. I told Ken that I was

surprised to read that he was just five foot four. Ken said that was actually pretty typical for Europeans of that era, adding, "Have you ever seen furniture or clothing from the seventeenth century? It's like miniaturized or kids' sized. Even the doorways were made for shorter people."

"You got that from your dreams?" I asked.

"Nope, Medieval Art History 356."

"But why were the Ho-Chunks noticeably taller according to François? They were obviously contemporaries," I wondered.

"I don't know, but I'd bet the average Ho-Chunk, hell, every tribe, had a better diet than the average European of that time."

We decided that it was a good time to take a break and run over to library to look for old photos. Ken said he remembered driving past a library in Trempealeau and that was probably the closest one. When we got there, we asked the librarian for the old photo section. She walked us down to the "valuable collections" in the lower level.

Halfway down the stairs Ken wondered out loud, "Why would you put the 'valuable collections' in the basement when we're less than two hundred yards from the Mississippi River?"

The librarian shrugged and asked us what we were looking for. We told her we were interested in old photos of the Pederson farm in Galesville. Incredibly she said, "Sorry, that farm is not in the collection."

"You know your collection by heart?" Ken asked.

"There are only forty-five old photographs, mostly from glass plate negatives. It's not hard to recall what we have there. What are you looking for?" She asked.

"We're interested in the outbuilding configuration of the homesteads of that era," Ken answered.

I looked at Ken with a bit of surprise at his concise summary of our interest.

"Well, perhaps seeing a sampling of contemporary farmsteads from the region will give you an idea of the customary buildings and their approximate locations on the land. Will that work for you?"

"Sure will. That's a great idea," Ken said. Adding after the librarian scurried out of sight, "At least we won't waste the drive down here."

Before I could respond to Ken's statement the librarian reappeared with a cardboard box, which she set on the table.

"I think you will find some useful pictures here. But if you don't, let me know and I will try later dates."

"Do we need white gloves?" I asked.

"No. Just please try to hold the pictures on the edges. I'll be working in the back. Call if you need me."

"Thanks, we will," I said.

Ken and I sat side by side so we could both see each picture at the same time. After the third picture it was clear that Dad was right. The customary farm building layout of western Wisconsin at the turn of the twentieth century included a smokehouse and outhouse east of the main house.

Ken thought the logic was that with prevailing westerly winds, the east side location would keep the smell and smoke generated in those two structures from wafting to the farmhouse.

We were convinced that the depressions we found were indeed precisely what my dad thought they were. It was disappointing but at least we didn't waste any more time on this dead end.

We thanked the librarian, left Trempealeau, and drove north to the Mountain in the River. Ken wanted to see the bluff for himself.

We parked and made our way up the winding path through the walnut forest to the top of the bluff overlooking the Mississippi River. I was happy Ken was going to see this, knowing how important it was for me to know the nightmares had a basis in reality. Ken had joked about "Frenchie," but his manic and obsessive painting, haunting murmurs and nightmares were just as disturbing as mine. But I wasn't sure if he viewed his delusions as more of a nuisance or if they shook him to the core as mine did to me.

We reached the top and walked to a rail fence facing north. Ken looked out at the point just as I had with my dad a month earlier. He took a deep breath, but didn't say anything. I looked up. He was crying. I hugged him.

After a few minutes of just looking out at the island, I asked if he'd like to stay. He just shook his head, and side-by-side we started down to the car.

It was halfway back to his farm before Ken was ready to talk.

"There weren't any boulders. I didn't think I'd take it so hard."

I nearly spit out the swallow of soda I just took, laughing. I wiped my mouth, "So that was it," I said, playing along with his charade.

Getting back to the gravity of the experience, Ken said, "Seeing the *actual* bluff that has been in my nightmares, after all that time of me questioning my grip on reality, was ... well, one of the most powerful emotions I have ever felt."

"It was for me, too. I'm glad we went," I said

Ken reached for my hand, held it briefly, "Thanks for bringing me. I can't believe it was just down the road from my farm all this time. I had no idea."

After another minute or two of silence he reached over and turned on the radio. Just static. He reached for the tuner. "Sometimes I can pick up a channel out of Minneapolis."

Sure enough, static turned to voices, then static; finally just a voice giving the weather, then saying, "Now from the top of the charts, John Denver's 'Country Roads.'"

"If I hear that song one more time, I think I'll puke!" Ken said.

"What do you like?"

"Anything by the Stones, Three Dog Night, or Janis Joplin." Then he broke into a very animated but atonal rendition of "Take another little piece of my heart ...!"

150

Once his channeling of Ms. Joplin stopped, I said, "I like that song too, but if you're thinking of starting a band, you may want to stick to painting."

"Let's see, you don't like my paintings, my singing stinks, you don't like anything. Geez there's no pleasing this woman."

"Well, I like you."

I waited for reciprocation, but none came.

"So, tell me about your family, Willa."

"Not really much to say. We're a typical nondescript clan. My dad's a partner in a logging and lumbering business. Mom worked at a farmers' co-op till my brothers were born. My brother Mike is four years older than I am and an accountant. He got back from Vietnam two and a half years ago, after eighteen months over there. He came back different, more sullen. If you ask him a question about the war he'll answer briefly, but he said that the booby traps, not knowing friend from enemy, indiscriminate killing of civilians on both sides, plus the things he won't talk about, took a toll. He and his wife, Joanie, have one kid and one on the way. I just love Joanie. She's like a sister. We can always tell what the other is thinking, it's freaky. Brother Pete is two years older than I am, just got married and works for my dad. He took his chances with the draft lottery and lucked out last year. So at least he won't have to go in. After the boys were born, I think I came along as a 'miscalculation.' My mom doted over me as her only daughter. Dad seemed a little out of his element with me. He was mostly around men his whole life. What about you?"

"Older sister, Kathy, lives with her boyfriend in Rochester. Has a pretty good job at IBM. Don't see her much since I went underground. My old man's a gung-ho ex-marine, former high school jock, crew cut and all. Can't stand the sight of me. I'm the opposite of what he wanted in a son. Thinks artists are fags, and that I'm a traitor to the country, a disgrace to the family, a dredge of society."

"What about your mom?"

"Tough question. The old man has her so intimidated and browbeaten she's afraid to say boo. I think she has your typical mother's instincts, but the old man's influence stifles 'em."

"Doesn't sound like you get much help from the family."

"My mom sends a few bucks once in a while. Don't really need the money though. Bud, Kathy's boyfriend, is my biggest customer. He's tapped into some IBMers, sells a shitload of weed, and we both make a ton of money. About the only time I get to see Kathy is when they come down to make a buy," Ken said.

"What does your family think of your visions and nightmares?"

"My old man thought I was pretty fucked up before, and wouldn't give a shit even if he knew about it. I didn't tell my mom either, she worries about everything. Except for the others that lived here, the few I've told don't believe me, so I just keep it to myself. Like I said, I never smoked weed before Frenchie got into my head. Smokin' is the only way I have been able to deal with it. It's so easy to grow that I figured it was a good way to keep myself supplied and make a few bucks. I was afraid that getting a job would blow my cover and there aren't many other ways to make money."

24

Once back at Ken's, I meandered from room to room looking at his paintings. Stacked in a corner of one of the bedrooms were several I hadn't seen before. I could hear Ken's hard steps walking up the wooden stairs. I called to him, "What are these pictures stacked in the bedroom of?"

"Don't remember. It's been awhile," he called back.

When he joined me, I gestured to the corner with the paintings. The electric company crew down the street had started up their chainsaws again and it was hard to converse without speaking loudly above the din.

"Oh those! Painted them about a year or so ago. Recurring image *de jour.*"

The first picture was of a cavern or pit in what looked like the side of a hill and, like most of the others, was black, charcoal, and other shades of grays.

The next painting was different—vivid in color. The yellow, red, and orange hues were a stark contrast to the others.

"What's this?" I asked.

"Just another hole."

"Well, it looks different to me. It looks like an abstract fall woods scene with colorful leaves on the ground and trees. That doesn't look like the other holes to me, that looks like a hole in a tree. What do you think?"

"Well, it could be. I hadn't thought about it that way, but it could be a forest floor and tree trunk with a hole at ground level."

I was still shouting when I realized the sawing had stopped. Lowering my voice I said, "Maybe he isn't buried in the ground at all."

"Would you like some lunch? I'm starving," Ken said.

"Sure, what've you got?"

"Bologna sandwiches is the best I can do," Ken said.

"Actually, that sounds pretty good to me," and I meant it.

Ken began to clean off the kitchen table. Seeing that the task he faced was formidable, I suggested that we eat on the porch.

"Okay. I'll make the sandwiches, you can wait on the porch. Let me know if Frenchie gets too loud to sit out there," Ken said.

I agreed and went out and sat on the steps of the front porch. It was relatively quiet except for the noise from the electric crew as they went about their job of cutting into smaller segments and gathering the limbs they had just trimmed. They were cutting any branches that were too near or overhanging the electric wires strung along the road. They had been working their way down the road and were nearly in front of Ken's property. It was a beautiful late summer afternoon and it felt nice to just sit and relax on the porch, despite the occasional annoying sawing sounds.

"Here ya go," Ken said, handing me a plate with a sandwich and a *pickle?*

"Thanks. You have pickles in your refrigerator?"

"No. When the others were still here, we grew a lot of vegetables and we canned them. The pickles are in the fruit cellar, along with some peppers and tomatoes. The only canned stuff left are the pickles. It'll take another year or two before I'm able to get through the last five jars. Do you want a beer or a glass of water? That's all I've got."

"I'll have a beer, thanks. The pickle's a nice touch."

Ken returned with two Chief Oshkosh beers. We clicked bottles and each took a swig.

"I can't remember the last time I had a bologna sandwich, pickle, and beer, but this sure hits the spot," I said.

We had just started talking about the paintings I had looked at before Ken offered to make sandwiches, when we saw one of the electric company crew walking up Ken's driveway.

"Hi. You the owner?" he asked.

"Yeah, why?" Ken asked.

"Just wanted to let you know we're done for the day. We got a few of the smaller branches down today, but when we come back early next week we will be taking one or two good sized branches off that tree in front. The tree's within ten feet of the road and on city property, but some of the branches are going to fall onto your lawn. Just wanted to give you a heads up. Let me show you which ones we're going to cut."

"Look, I'm kind of busy right now."

He looked skeptically at Ken sitting there with a beer in his hand.

"It'll just take a minute. I don't want you to park your vehicle too close."

In an exasperated tone, Ken said, "Okay, fine."

We put our plates down and, carrying our beers, the two of us followed the guy to the huge tree on the road in front of Ken's farm.

While we walked, I asked the crewman, "Why does the city own the land ten feet from the road? We're blocks from town. It's so rural," I wondered.

"City planned for development out here in the early fifties. Figured they'd run water and sewer and maybe put in sidewalks. This was supposed to be all residential by now. The only problem was nobody wanted to develop it. Well, it'll be ready when they do. Okay, look up. See them two big branches? They have to come down. We got a couple of smaller ones on the road side, but those big branches will take a couple of hours and it's too late in the day to start on them."

"Okay. Thanks for showing us. We'll be sure to stay clear. When are you coming back, again?" asked Ken.

"Monday or Tuesday," the crewman said.

"Well, have a good weekend. See you then," Ken said.

I was struck by an odd feeling. It was a powerful emotional response to the smell of that newly cut wood. Not any cut wood. Working with my dad and brothers as a kid, we were always around sawed wood of all different species. But this particular smell was prominent during a couple of the submersions. It meant something important, but I didn't know what. Ken and I walked back up the steps and onto his porch. We sat down and watched the Wisconsin Electric Company truck drive off, and we resumed our lunch.

Ken asked, "Where were we before the interruption? Oh yeah, the yellow picture. Maybe he's buried in or near a tree. Well, that's fine but where the hell do you expect to find a three or four hundred-year-old tree? Hell, it would have to be older than that to be big enough for Frenchie to be buried or trapped in it a couple hundred years ago."

"Oh my gosh! How could we be so stupid! Ken, that's it! He wasn't buried alive in the ground, but inside a hollow tree. We've been thinking about this all wrong. He's in that basswood on the road!" I exclaimed.

25

I grabbed his hand and nearly dragged Ken across his front yard to the basswood.

"He's in here!" I put my arms on the trunk stretching around a fourth of its girth. Ken did the same, grasping my hand with one of his. The tree murmured. I don't know how else to describe it.

"Do you feel that?!"

"I sure as hell do!" Ken answered.

"We've got to cut it down!" I told him.

"We can't. This is city property. Don't you remember what that guy just told us?"

"Screw the city. I'll be happy to plead guilty and suffer the consequences for 'premeditated murder' of a city tree. Let's get started."

"Watch out city! The pushy broad's in action mode!" Ken laughed. "Don't you want to call your dad down here? This sure looks like a job that's right up his alley."

"No. There's no telling how long it will take him to get down here and if I'm wrong, well, I hate to waste his time and further tax his patience with his crazy daughter. No, let's do this. Don't you have a chainsaw in the barn?"

"Yup. I'll get it."

Ken returned with an old, beat-up chainsaw. I stood there watching him for several minutes fiddle-fuck around with it trying to get it started until I couldn't watch anymore.

"Ken, you keep flooding it. It'll never start," I said.

"You want to give it a try?" he said with a little sarcasm.

"Yes. You're talkin' to a logger's kid here. I know a thing or two about chainsaws. First, you don't leave the choke all the way out after the second pull. That's why you keep flooding it. Push it in about halfway after that, like this."

I gave the cord a pull—sputtering and blue smoke, but no ignition.

"Your gas-oil mix is too rich. We need to add some gas. Do you have any chain lubricant? What's in there won't last our first four-inch cut."

"Yes sir! I mean ma'am!" Ken saluted me and ran toward the barn, laughing all the way.

I didn't think any of this was funny.

He returned with a two-gallon gas can and black plastic bottle and set each next to the saw on the ground. The gas can didn't have much in it, but it was enough to fill the saw's tank. The plastic bottle didn't have a label on it, but I smelled it and agreed with Ken that it was chain lubricant.

After the third pull it started briefly, the fourth pull did it. The blue smoke dissipated after a few seconds and the saw ran smoothly. I went right to work.

It took five minutes of wielding the saw before my adrenaline rush subsided, my arms were getting heavy, and I was exhausted. I worked the chain out of the ten-inch-deep cut I had made on the yard side of the tree, shut it down, and plopped down with my back against the tree, which seemed to be vibrating. Ken sat down next to me.

"The tree's still humming. I was pretty sure you weren't going to stop until you toppled, limbed, and cut it into firewood. I'll take the next shift, if you trust me with *my* saw," Ken said.

"Yeah, I know I can get a little focused, but this is just too damned important to let it go unresolved, even for a couple of days. Let's work in shifts," I said.

"That's a good idea, and I feel the same way about getting this resolved. Just remind me to never piss you off, okay?"

We got back up not because I wanted to, but because

the tree was vibrating so much it was uncomfortable sitting against it. Based on the tree's lean, I showed Ken where I thought we should make the deepest notched cut and where we would cut through from the other side. This would make sure it fell diagonally away from the house, the power lines, and the road. I've seen this done a hundred times and was confident with the plan. Ken went right to work.

He was making a lot more progress than I did. Within fifteen minutes he expanded the first cut to a couple of feet deep. Then we heard a "pinging" sound, like the chain hit something hard.

Ken worked the chain out of the cut, turned off the saw and set it down.

"I must have hit a rock or something."

"That's kind of high up in the trunk for a rock. Who knows? A couple hundred years of frosts and thaws could push a stone up that high, especially if there's a cavity," I said.

"Your turn, Willa, I'm beat."

"Okay. I'll cut the bottom half of the notch. I don't want to ruin the saw by banging it into that rock."

Before long I hit the rock just below the point Ken did, coming up at a thirty-degree angle from the first straight cut. I feebly kicked at the triangular block trying to dislodge it. Ken must have known the futility of my attempt and ran off to the barn. He returned with a sledgehammer.

His first swing with the sledgehammer hit the widest point of the block squarely and moved it six inches to the side. His second whack sent the wedge flying out, leaving a deep V cut to the middle of the trunk. A small piece of what looked like a blue-hued granite rock was visible.

"Now what?" Ken asked.

"Good question. I think we need to cut past the midpoint to be sure the weight shift is away from the road and toward the side yard. With that rock there, I don't know. I guess we should cut another smaller V block on the east side. We'll cut till we hit the rock and hope that the combination of the two cuts are deep enough to get the tree to topple in that direction."

With a nod, Ken restarted the saw and began to cut a second overlapping wedge.

The second wedge was much smaller, and Ken was able to finish it in a couple of minutes before hitting the rock again.

He knocked the smaller wedge out on his first swing. We could see the blue rock again, but this time a hollow part was visible.

"That explains the rock being up so high, I guess," Ken said. He stuck his head into the V-shaped cut and tried to peer into the hollow. "Can't see anything," he said.

It was getting late in the afternoon but neither of us had any interest in stopping.

My turn. The saw started up reluctantly. I began the straight cut on the road side of the tree, which was intended to eventually cause the tree to lean toward the wedge and topple over. Anyway, that was our plan.

Halfway through, my arms weakened and I had to hand off cutting to Ken. He continued cutting to the rock, this time from the other side. We expected the tree to fall. It didn't.

"Shit. We're all the way through to the rock. Isn't this thing supposed to fall?" Ken said.

"Yeah. I don't understand. Well, the only thing I can think of is to drive a wedge into the cut you just made on the road side. Hopefully that will tip the tree's center of gravity enough to topple it. You don't happen to have an eight-inch iron wedge, do you?"

"No, but I think I have something that'll work." And with that he ran off to the barn again.

I could hear the tree murmuring. "Hurry!" I called to Ken.

He returned quickly, and proudly showed me a fistful of railroad spikes. "These should work."

"Railroad spikes? They're perfect! Where did you get these?"

"We'd dig some up every time we tilled. Must have been an old rail line back there at one time."

26

Using the sledgehammer, we drove the first spike deep into the saw cut and waited. Nothing. The second spike. Nothing. The third spike. Nothing ... then something. There was a slight movement at the very top of the tree. The weight of the giant basswood was beginning to shift.

With each breath we could see the momentum build, and the tree leaned in the direction we planned. But the trunk began to twist, farther and farther until it headed right toward Ken's house.

I looked at Ken looking at me. "Oops," I said.

We watched helplessly as the tree picked up speed as it fell to the ground. It bounced briefly and came to rest next to the house. One huge limb hit the roof on the porch and ripped off the gutter and fascia board.

"Ken, I'm so sorry. I thought I had this." I hugged him hoping to make a little amend.

"If that tree had hit my house it could have done up to seventy-five dollars, maybe even eighty dollars damage!" Ken said in mock indignation. Then added, "Anyway, I blame that one on the electric company. That was one of the branches that guy told us they were going to cut. If they hadn't knocked off early today, it wouldn't have been there."

I appreciated his attempts to ease how terrible I felt and looked at Ken to say so.

But he wasn't looking at the house any longer and had a strange expression on his face—astonishment. I followed his line of sight away from the house and to the stump of the tree behind us. Looking like he was hiding behind a three-foot high jagged side of the stump that pulled off as the tree toppled, was the emaciated figure of a man, looking upward, hollow eye-sockets and mouth agape as though frozen in mid-scream. His skin was a teal blue streaked with deep greens. His clothing was preserved well enough to be recognizable, and appeared to be a justaucorps coat over military-issue pants with a silk stripe on the sides, home spun shirt, and fur cap tilted to the side. The clothing looked three sizes too large draped over his desiccated frame. What appeared to be a musket was at his side, barrel up, reaching his shoulder where a metal powder horn hung at his side.

"François, you sonofabitch," Ken exclaimed in awe.

27

Ken and I sat on the ground mesmerized, looking up at François' body. Since visiting Ken's farm, this was the first and only time there was silence in his front yard. No, humming, murmurs, or voices.

I was feeling an amalgamation of emotions: relief, exhaustion, fascination, giddiness, and as Ken's face expressed when he first gazed on François—astonishment. We actually did it!

I grabbed Ken's hand and waist and led him on a victory polka dance around the stump. We laughed out of exhilaration at having found François, and the silly spectacle we must have been. We danced our last victory lap and stood next to each looking again at François, and Ken said, "So the sonofabitch talks to us, haunts us, torments the shit out of us for months, and *now* he doesn't have the decency to say thank you?"

Then he added, "You know, I'm getting a clear vision of what happened. He climbed into this hollowed trunk, running from that band of Fox Indians. They picked up his trail after he waded through the swamp from the island. They were closing in on him. He could hear their hoops and hollers getting nearer and nearer. His lungs were burning. This tree was his last best hope to escape. He pushed himself up until he was snuggly nestled here. He knew immediately he made a mistake. He couldn't budge, struggled and died.

Near the end, he wasn't sure whether it was real or if he was just dreaming it all. What a shitty way to die."

"How do you know this?" I asked.

"How did we know any of it? Seeing the hole, him, his clothes, I don't know, but it triggered memories. Somehow, he communicated it. Just like I was drawn right to this farm. Of all the places I could have found an old farmstead, I found this place. It always had to be this place. When my buddies wanted to look at other farms, I dug my heels in for this place. That's not a coincidence. He led me here. Just like he led you to that bluff. I hated this guy. But you know, I really feel sorry for him now. Can you imagine the horror of that moment when he realized he couldn't get back out of the tree? What do you do? Cry out for help? To whom? No one around except the people trying to kill you and they'd have to be right next to the tree to hear. Pray?" Ken said.

"Based on what you and I dreamt, heard, and envisioned, he must have done all of those things. You're right, what a horrible way to die. I'd bet before he died, he went through exactly what I went through in the sensory deprivation tank—no light, complete silence except for your own screams, not being able to tell thoughts and dreams from reality. Except I could scream and immediately get pulled out. He couldn't. He could scream all he wanted. There was no extraction, no return to reality or senses. That's probably the common denominator for us. We both entered that same discombobulated state of mind where we couldn't tell reality from dreams. That's how we connected. That's why we got stuck with him," I said.

"Let's see if he has papers or identification," Ken said.

I wanted nothing to do with getting any closer, much less rifling through his pockets, so I said nothing. Ken rose and gingerly stepped up onto the flat side of the stump, pulling himself up by grabbing hold of the jagged piece of trunk. With François' lower legs still held fast within the stump Ken towered over him. The silhouette looked like an adult standing with a child.

Ken must have been way past having any fear of François because he stood over the body and casually, but carefully, patted the side of the jacket pockets, but found no identification.

"He's petrified! We didn't hit a rock, it was him. I can see where the chainsaw cut his pant leg and dinged his leg. I think he looks like he's smiling."

Then Ken reached around the musket and pulled out what appeared to be a folded document from a breast pocket inside the man's coat. Holding the paper between two fingers as though it may disintegrate any second, Ken turned and stepped down from the stump.

"Let's go inside where it's light enough to read this," Ken said.

Ken pushed the paints, brushes, containers, and trash away, clearing two spots at his kitchen table. Some fell unnoticed onto the floor. We sat next to each other while he unfolded the document.

The heavy creases and stains made it difficult, but not impossible, to see the faded writing. We read it aloud together, our voices as one.

Decree, New France, 3 juin 1712.
Let it be known to all. Under the power, authority and benevolence of King Louis XIV of France and the auspices of the Governor of New France, it is hereby decreed that Fusilier François Renaulti is granted the privilege to serve the King as Couriers de Bois, to mark, survey and assert the claim of the Crown of the King and in the name of the King and of France, on all territories to the west of the riviere mississippi. These lands are claimed and rightly endowed to France by the authority of the King and in the eyes of God.

"Well, that settles it. There's no doubt now, it's him alright. I need a drink," Ken said.

"I could use several. Let's go out or get some booze. Your

Chief Oshkosh stash is low and I don't do your other stash," I said.

"I'll get some booze. There really isn't a place to celebrate for forty miles and I sure as hell don't want to drive home loaded. I can't risk getting a parking ticket, much less a DUI. I'd be on my way to 'Nam or they'd throw my ass in a federal pen. There's a liquor store just south of town. I'll be back in fifteen minutes. Any requests?"

"Yeah, booze. Do you want me to kick in anything?" I asked.

"Nah. This one's on Donny."

Ken left immediately. I headed back out to the tree and plopped down where Ken and I sat in front of François. It was getting dark, but I couldn't take my eyes off him. I thought that finding François would provide the answers. But there are only more questions. Is this it? Are the nightmares and visions going to stop? All this bullshit I went through and it's over, just like that? What do you do with the body of a two hundred and fifty-year-old French guy? What does François want? Do I let Dan know we found him? Do I gloat and do an "I told you so, asshole"?' What about the depression and episodes of obsessive manic behavior and sleep deprivation? Will they stop too? What about Ken? We were drawn together because of François. Now what? I really like him, but does he want to get back to life as ... as whatever he is? Does he like me? Will his chick come back to hippie paradise and pick up where she left off? Well, François?

I sat on the ground and just looked up at François, silhouetted against the sky. He was frozen in time looking up, jaws agape. After some time, it occurred to me that Ken was right, it did look like François was smiling.

Headlights were coming up the road. Ken was back from the booze run.

28

"I thought a little classy French brandy would be in order," Ken said, holding up the bag proudly.

He had to coax the cork out of the bottle with a fork after his short search for a corkscrew proved futile. We clicked glasses "cheers" and did a shot. "Hey, what about François? Let's give him a little brandy, too," Ken suggested.

"Why not? Somehow, someway, he's got to be in a celebrating mood. Maybe that'll bribe him into finally leaving us the hell alone," I said.

Together we walked out into the dark, across the front yard past the shadow of the giant fallen tree and to the stump. Ken stepped up and stood on the stump next to the petrified remains. He raised his glass *"Viva la François."* After I raised mine and repeated the toast, Ken poured a small amount of brandy into the open mouth of the body of François.

"I hope you're happy, François," Ken said.

Satisfied with ourselves for our impromptu tribute, we resumed our celebrating inside.

"So, who do we call to take charge of François?" I asked.

"Got me. Maybe the coroner. If there's a body, we probably have to call the police, too. The police are the last people I want creeping around here, but I'm not sure we have a choice."

"I'll call them both tomorrow morning. You can stay inside if you need to. I'll explain this."

"Really? You're going to explain why the hell you chopped down a city tree, onto my property, and just by some wild chance, there's a French guy inside?"

"Yup. I'm just going to tell them the truth."

"I've got to hear this," Ken said.

I crashed on the couch around midnight. Ken went back out to the stump for one last visit. I fell asleep before he came back in.

29

I woke up around seven o'clock the next morning. Ken was already up and sitting on the steps of his porch.

"Hey."

"Oh, hey. You were really sawin' 'em off in there so I thought I'd let you sleep. You want to run over to the diner for breakfast?"

"That was the best night's sleep I've had in months, and breakfast sounds great. But there's one thing I want to do before we leave," I said.

After getting dressed, I gathered up the journal and walked out to the stump and leaned it against François' leg.

Ken watched me from the truck. I hopped in and said, "Just returning the journal to its rightful owner."

At the diner we took Ken's favorite booth and were immediately greeted by who I assume was Ken's favorite waitress, Suzie.

We must have looked like hell, because the first thing Suzie said, with as much disdain as she could muster, was, "Big night last night?"

"You could say that," Ken answered. "We need coffee and OJ. We'll order when you get back. Oh, Suzie, can you bring us the phone book, too?" he added.

"Sure thing," Suzie glared at me as she turned to leave.

Ken ignored her. I was happy she was miffed, even if it wasn't what she was implying.

"After breakfast I'll call the coroner and ask if we need to call the police too, considering the obvious age of the body," I said.

Ken nodded.

Suzie returned with a coffee pot, mugs, two large glasses of orange juice on a tray and a phone book under her arm. She emptied the tray and then set the phone book on the table. "What'll you have?" and she took our orders.

After we finished eating, I looked up the Trempealeau County Coroner's Office number in the phone book, fished through my purse for a quarter and called from the phone on the wall by the diner's bathrooms. After seven rings, I had just about given up hope when a woman answered, "Coroner's office, our hours are nine to five weekdays. Please call back then."

"No, no, please don't hang up. I have found a body. It's in a tree east of Galesville and I have no idea who to call. Can you help me?"

"You have a human body in a tree, is that what I heard you say?"

"Yes ma'am."

"Do you have any idea how it got up in that tree?"

"The body isn't up in the branches of the tree, the body is inside a hollow within the tree."

"When you find a body, you need to call the police immediately, Miss. If the police want the coroner, they will call us."

"The reason I called your office first is that it's pretty obvious the body has been there for a long, long time. This isn't a crime scene, it's more an archeology find."

"Who am I speaking with?" she asked.

"I'm Willa Heinlein."

"Well Miss Heinlein, what makes you think the body has been there 'a long, long time'?"

"Well, it's petrified, has a rusted musket, and a letter in a pocket dated 1712."

"I will call the coroner at home and see what he would like to do. In the meantime, you should call the police. Regardless of the age of the body, this is police business. Where can I reach you, Miss?"

I read her the phone number printed on the circular label stuck to the center of the dial on the phone. "I am calling from a pay phone at a diner. You can leave a message with the diner staff if I'm not here. The address where the body is ... actually, I don't know the address, but it's the last house at the end of East Avenue in Galesville. There's a 100 foot basswood on the ground there, you can't miss it."

"Either I or the coroner will get back to you. Thanks for calling. Goodbye."

"We have to call the police, Ken."

"I knew it."

"When they come, why don't you stay in the background, maybe on the porch. I will only call you over if I need you. Is that okay with you?" I asked.

"Of course it is," Ken said.

"Good. I understand the risk that you take. I said I'd take responsibility for cutting down the tree and I will. It really doesn't matter which of us explains what happened to the police, so it may as well be me," I said.

"I'm not trying to hang you out to dry here, Willa. It's just ..."

"Come on, Ken. There is no reason we should let this lead to even more problems for you. For heaven's sake, my tree felling skills nearly demolished your house. Let's finish our coffee and see if the coroner calls back in the next few minutes. If not, I'll call the police," I said.

We finished our coffee. I called the police station. The officer who answered said the coroner had already called them and the sheriff was on the scene.

We hurried back to Ken's and saw the sheriff's squad and the clearly marked coroner's cars. They were already at the stump. I wasn't sure what I was going to say, but for better or worse, I would basically tell them exactly what happened.

"I'm Willa, I'm the one who called the coroner's office."

173

"Where you from, Willa?" the sheriff asked.

"I live in Madison, but I'm from Sawyer County."

"What brings you here?"

"I am visiting a friend. He lives in that house," I said, pointing to Ken on his porch.

"Who cut this tree down?"

"I did, officer."

"I found that old journal, which led me to believe a man was in this tree." I pointed to the journal I had leaned against François' leg that morning, then continued. "I know it sounds incredible, but I was confident I'd find him there, and sure enough, there he is."

"I see him," he said sternly, "but you just can't go around cutting down city trees because you have a hunch. Are you an archeologist?"

"An amateur archeologist. I'm a graduate student in psychology."

"And how do you know your friend who lives here?"

"I met him and imposed my theory about a guy in a tree once I had narrowed the search to this tree in front of his house."

"You're either unbelievably lucky or one hell of an amateur archeologist. Either way, I have to write you a $168 ticket for damage to city property. Also, that tree has to be removed within a week or the city will do it and send you the bill. You also caused property damage. If the home owner files an insurance claim, there needs to be an accident report. The report will cite you as the cause of the damage. I will need to see your driver's license and get your contact information."

"Yes sir, I understand." I handed him my license. "By the way, officer, what happens to the body now?"

"I'm not sure. When we find skeletal remains that old, they're usually from Indian burials and their tribe claims the remains. This is kind of a new one on me. But the coroner has a protocol he follows and will keep the body for a couple of months to give kin a chance to claim it. If no one calls, then it's up to him."

The sheriff finished the paperwork, handed me the ticket and had me sign the property damage report. "You don't have your eye on any other trees in town do you, Miss?" he said, smiling for the first time.

"No sir. That was the only one," I said, smiling back.

"Well, that's good. I always figured I'd make a call on this farmhouse eventually, but I never thought it would be for something like this. You have yourself a good day, Miss."

30

Ken and I sat next to each other on the top step of his porch watching the coroner wrapping François in a sheet and placing the shrouded body into the back of the coroner's station wagon.

"Where do you think François would want to be buried?" I said.

"Don't know. Don't care. But I'll bet you have some thoughts on this," Ken said, bumping me with his shoulder.

"I was thinking about it. Maybe we should contact Canadian authorities and just let them know that François is at the coroner's office here. They may have some interest."

"That's a good idea. Send them a letter and they can do what they want. But I'm more interested in what we're going to do about that tree lying next to my house."

"Let's ask my dad or my brothers to come down and give us a hand. If they can, they will. If not, at least I can get a couple of heavy-duty saws from them."

"Not to change the subject but, what are you going to do about your PhD program?"

"Honestly, I don't know. I might have a chance to salvage it next semester, but it starts in a couple of weeks. Last semester was shot. My boyfriend and project professor thinks I'm crazy and dumped me a couple of weeks ago. I've got a year left to go, but I'm not sure I want a degree in psych anymore. I kind of soured on the field after my boyfriend, who is the most qualified psychologist I know, thought the only way to deal with my problem was to dope me up on anti-psychotic medication. So there's a lot to think about."

"The project professor is the douche bag, right?"

"Yup. Ken, you only overheard him talking for maybe five minutes and you nailed it. It took my dad an hour or so to come up with the same conclusion you did. What's wrong with me? It took me seven months. How did you size him up so fast?"

"All I noticed is that he didn't seem to listen to a word you said. You were telling him about your visions and I knew from my own experience what you said was completely credible. In fact, we just proved it. But he wasn't interested in anything you were saying. While you were talking, he seemed to be just thinking about what his rebuttal would be when you paused. That's what douche bags do in my world."

"I wasn't sure that I wasn't crazy though. I couldn't just dismiss Dan's take on this. I thought he cared about me. That he would use his expertise to help me through this. Instead he was trying to find a way to avoid embarrassment and get my data out of the research so he could get it published. I was just disappointed in him, that's all," I said, starting to lose it. "You know what's funny? That's exactly what my dad said, that he was disappointed in Dan."

"Are you okay, Willa?"

I nodded. Ken put his hand on mine.

"Dan is so smart, but it's book smart. He reads voraciously and remembers everything he reads. But there is little critical thinking going on. He just remembers what he reads about the issue and takes that position, because he has confidence that it must be right. Hell, even my un-inspiring take on Freud that got me into graduate school impressed him because he couldn't remember reading anything precisely on my interpretation. But my position was really pretty obvious, and certainly should have appeared that way to someone like him, a Doctor of Psychology. It's the same thing diagnosing my problem and when he talked to my dad about what's going on in Vietnam and on campus.

He refuses to think about issues beyond the prevailing attitude in the literature. Anyway, I finally see him the way you and my dad do. What are you going to do, Ken?"

"Don't know. When you told me what the sheriff said, that he figured he'd be making a visit here at some point, that's a little scary. I thought I was under the radar. Evidently not. I've got to come up with a plan B. But that draft thing won't be going away."

"You need to talk to my brother Pete. He knows the draft system. After my brother Mike went to 'Nam, my dad was ready to pay for Pete to go to Canada instead of getting drafted. Pete said he'd figure something out, and he did."

"I appreciate that offer, I really do. But there is no scamming the draft. My number is my number and as far as Uncle Sam is concerned, I'm a draft dodger. There really isn't much for your brother to figure out," Ken said.

"Well, never say never. I'll run over to the diner and call Peter first to try to get him to come down and help remove that tree. If he comes, talk to him if you want to. If he can't make it, I'll head home tonight and come back Monday with some equipment to help you with the tree. While I'm at the diner do you want me to pick something up to eat?"

"Sure. Surprise me."

31

"**P**izza!" I yelled when I arrived back at Ken's house.

"Great! Are we going to get some help with that tree?" Ken asked.

"Oh yeah. I talked to Peter. He can't wait to come, says basswoods that big are hard to find and worth some money, even with the first log hollow. If he can keep the saw logs, that'll pay for the trip and then some. He'll be here tomorrow morning with a couple of guys, flatbed, and log grabber. Do you mind if I spend one more night?"

"So you're getting used to these four-star accommodations, are you? Of course you can stay. Hey, your brother helping us out sure beats the hell out of me and you cutting it up, or paying the city to do it. It'll be nice to get that thing outta here. He can keep it all if he wants it, I sure have no use for it."

"I told Peter about your draft situation, too. He's going to think about it and if you'd like, you guys can talk about it."

"I appreciate it, but this is a rock and a hard place problem. I can't imagine that he'll be able to help, but I'm happy to talk with him."

We finished the pizza and our brandys. He excused himself and went upstairs, so I decided to take a walk. I didn't get far before it struck me how wonderful it was to be François-free. I hadn't had a vision or nightmare or that murmuring tinnitus since yesterday when we cut the tree down. I slept like a log—on Ken's lumpy, smelly couch no less. What a relief it was to be *normal* again! Except in my case *normal* means no job, struggling PhD program, and an expensive apartment I can't afford because I only worked for a few weeks this entire summer. Maybe Peter will have some ideas that will help me, too. I walked past a bakery not far from the diner and decided to buy a few pastries for breakfast and for Peter and his crew.

I got back, put the pastries away, and heard Ken coming down the stairs. I looked up and for an instant was startled. That wasn't Ken. It was clean-shaven Ken! A face I had never seen.

"Who is that 'unmasked man'?" I asked.

"I figured it was time to get rid of that thing. It reminded me of Frenchie. What do you think?" he said as he toweled off his still-wet hair from a shower.

"Give me a minute to adjust. I kind of liked that other guy." Actually, I think I like this one better. Face looks a little thin, but I can finally see his smile. Wearing just sweat pants and without his beard, he didn't look anything like a hippie toker. More like that guy on TV in the Schick razor commercial. Wow!

"I cleaned out the shower a little in case you wanted to use it, too. There's a towel and a clean sweat-suit on the sink if you want to use it."

"A shower would feel great, thanks." I went upstairs. He did clean out the shower, "a little." He cleans like my brothers cleaned—half-assed. Oh well, it's still the cleanest place in the house.

I finished and went downstairs. Ken was on the porch sitting in one of two chairs he took from the kitchen. I sat in the chair next to him.

"Felt good didn't it?" he asked.

I nodded, and smiled at Ken.

"I've been saving this for a special occasion," he said, reaching next to his chair and lifting up an open bottle of Merlot with two plastic cups upside down over the bottle's top.

"What are we celebrating? Your clean shower?"

"Sure, why not? But I was thinking more along the lines of celebrating a second day of not being crazy. It's so hard to believe that two years of this shit, and suddenly—poof—it's over. No fanfare, no warning, just over. And then there's this pushy broad that made it happen. There's no way I would have figured this out without your ... help. Help is the wrong word. Without your refusal to take no for an answer, your perseverance. You figured this out, I just came along for the ride. Thanks Willa." Ken leaned over and softly kissed my lips. Then he bent over and picked up the wine bottle and two plastic cups. He poured mine first and handed the cup to me. Then poured his and gently took my empty hand in his, and raised his glass.

"Cheers!"

"Yeah, cheers," I think I said. I was still in that kiss.

32

I woke up to engine noise and loud voices. I got up from the couch and looked out the kitchen window just as Ken rumbled down the stairs. "It's my brother. He likes to start early," I said.

We walked out onto the porch and waved to Peter. He waved back, finished what he was saying to his crew and walked across the lawn to us. He gave me hug, then turned, introduced himself to Ken and shook his hand.

"Hey, is that how Dad taught you to fell a tree?" Peter asked, making fun of my near disaster.

"I told the tree which direction to fall but it just wouldn't listen. Must be a male tree," I chided.

"Or a woman lumberjack," Peter retorted. "Doesn't look like the damage is too bad. Geez, that's a nice tree. That's the biggest basswood I've ever seen. It's a shame that first log is hollow. That's the money log, but basswood isn't as valuable as oak or maple. The wood is really soft for a hardwood and probably the reason it wasn't cut down before you two got to it."

"Are you going to make any money on the wood, Peter?" Ken said.

"Hell yes. Still looks to be around six hundred, maybe seven hundred board feet in the rest of it, that's pretty good."

"If the wood isn't valuable like oak or maple, who are you going to sell it to?" Ken asked.

"We can saw some of it up into blocks and sell it to a

decoy maker I know in Minneapolis. Being soft, basswood is easy to carve and perfect for decoys. The rest of it we'll cut into clapboard. They don't build with it much anymore, but there's still a demand for replacing pieces or matching siding after adding on a room or garage. We should have this cut up and loaded by noon. We're gonna have to leave the branches though. But we'll cut 'em up into firewood size bolts, pile those by the house, and pull the tops back into the field if that's okay," Pete said.

"You bet it's okay. I really appreciate you coming down here to help us with this," Ken said.

"Happy to do it."

"Can you stay for lunch?" I asked.

"Sure. I'll send the crew back when the logs are loaded, but I can stick around for lunch."

Peter went back to work. I wasn't sure what we would do for lunch, but I got the pastries out, kept a couple for Ken and me, and brought the rest to Peter and his crew.

By eleven that morning the chainsaws stopped. The flatbed had five, ten-foot logs chained down and a cord and a half of firewood bolts stacked against the house. As one of the crew was finishing up, he straightened and reattached the gutter and fascia board on the porch that were mangled when the tree grazed it.

"You didn't have to do that," Ken said to Peter.

"No problem. While we're here why not finish it up?" Peter said.

Peter walked over to his crew, gave them instructions on what to do with the logs when they got back to the mill and then walked across the yard to join us on the porch.

Ken took another chair out of the kitchen and set it on the porch next to ours.

"You guys go ahead and talk, I'll make some lunch." I went into the kitchen to make our bologna sandwiches, but left the door open so I could hear what they were talking about.

"So I understand you and the draft board aren't seeing eye to eye," Peter said.

"You could say that. My draft number is ninety-seven and I'm screwed. So, I made myself hard to find."

"Yeah, I went through that, too. My number was 121 and they were drafting all the way up to 180 or 190. The only other way to avoid the draft is to be unfit. Either you need a doctor to write you a letter sayin' you'll be dead in a month, or you say you're a homo. But sayin' that will stick with you the rest of your life."

"No, I couldn't say that, either. How'd you get out of going to 'Nam then?"

"I had a deferment but knew I would lose it in a year or two. So I waited out the first year because that was right after Tet, and they were drafting like crazy. But by October of 1970, they were only at 104 and it looked like they were slowing down inductions. I decided I'd go for it and reported to my draft board. That made me vulnerable until the end of the year. Once January rolled around, they never got to my number, so that was that, my obligation was met. So how far are you in the process?"

"I got the first letter telling me to report to my draft board and get a date for my physical. That's when I left Minnesota," Ken said.

"You know you might be in the same boat I was in last year. Your number is ninety-seven? Well, they're only at sixty-eight right now. Nixon is getting so much shit for the war, I don't think you're gonna see a big push for more draftees between now and year end. This may be a good time to take your shot."

"I don't know. I'm AWOL as far as the draft board is concerned. That's a felony. Look what they're doin' to Mohammad Ali for God's sake. They threw him in jail. Mohammad Ali! No, I'm either goin' right to federal prison or 'Nam. Those are my options and they're both bummers."

"Well, maybe not. A buddy of mine moved from the U.P. to work in Stevens Point. Michigan was all pissy about him not reporting. But because his residence changed, and as long as he was registered in Wisconsin, they backed off. That could work for you."

"I don't see how. I'm a felon. They're not going to forgive and forget."

"But they're also bureaucrats. They're not after you personally, they want their paperwork in order. So give it to them ... you know what I'd do? Send a letter to your Minnesota draft board and ask them why you haven't heard from them, since you're ready to enter the draft. Give them your address here. Then register in Wisconsin. Tell them you moved here, and since you never heard anything from them in Minnesota, you went ahead and registered here. This is your permanent residence anyway. They just want to be sure you are in the draft. Hell, every out-of-state college kid has a change of residence and new draft board. I'd bet half are late registering and most of those are late in notifying their draft boards. They're not all going to jail."

"What if the Wisconsin board contacts Minnesota?"

"Great. Minnesota tells them they lost track of you when you moved, but you contacted them to let them know you're a Wisconsin resident and were going to register in Wisconsin now. Wisconsin says you are registered and a resident and are entered into this year's lottery. Everybody's happy."

"What if they draft like crazy the last two months of the year?"

"Then you're screwed. But that's no different than where you are right now anyway. At least this way you have a *chance* to become an upright citizen again. Otherwise, you'll be looking over your shoulder your whole life or you'll need to go to Mexico or Canada."

"Man, it would be cool to have this off my back. But I've got to think this through."

"I understand. Hey, my dad was ready to send me to Canada if I wanted to go. He felt that with my brother Mike already serving a tour in 'Nam and him volunteering for

World War II, our family's military obligation was fulfilled. What does your dad think about this?"

"That I should be dragged into the town square and shot. Only a commie wouldn't fight for America. He's ex-military too, but he's all gung-ho. Kind of has a Joe McCarthy communist paranoia mindset—anyone who protests is a commie and there's a commie behind every tree. We haven't talked much the last couple of years."

"Lunch is ready." I handed Ken and Peter each a plate with a sandwich and pickle. I made myself half a sandwich. When I realized how in shape Ken was, seeing him in just sweat pants after his shower, I thought a half-sandwich was enough for me. I should probably take a walk later, too.

"I didn't mean to interrupt. You guys were really hammering out a strategy."

"Well, maybe. It's kind of a big risk," Ken said.

"It didn't sound like that to me, from what I heard. It was more a matter of gaining an opportunity with the worst-case scenario being that you're in the same place you are now—a fugitive," I said.

"That's how I see it too, Ken," Peter said.

"Are you two ganging up on me?"

"No. You're the only one that can decide. Peter and I aren't trying to be cavalier with your future. It's gotta be your call," I said.

Peter finished his last bite of sandwich, thanked us for lunch and the pastries, and got up to leave. I hugged him hard and thanked him for being a great "big brother." He shook Ken's hand, wished him luck, and left.

33

I walked with Ken around the house as he admired the work Peter and his crew had done. Then we sat on the porch and talked for a while. I told Ken I wanted to take a walk, then pack up my few things and leave before it got dark.

Ken asked if I would mind if he came along on my walk. Of course I didn't. Instead of heading west down the road toward town as I had before, Ken led me south. We walked on the road past the tree line the electric company crew trimmed the week before, and to a rutted dirt road winding toward a wood lot.

"I used to jog this trail every day when I first got here. But it's been a while," Ken said.

Once we crossed the field and reached the woods it was just like the old logging roads back home. We meandered through the oaks up and down steep moraines and along a fast-flowing creek. It was beautiful. We talked and laughed a lot, and I was surprised when we emerged from the woods and saw the back of Ken's barn and farmhouse. The late summer sun was already setting behind the trees.

"What time is it?" I asked.

"I don't know, maybe six-thirty or seven."

"We walked for two hours?" I said incredulously.

"Probably. That's a five-and-a-half-mile loop. With the hills, it can take a couple hours."

Once inside, I plopped myself down on the couch and realized how tired I was from the fresh air and all those miles.

Ken sat down next to me, gave me a peck on the temple and said, "Thanks Willa. I didn't realize how much I missed ... *normal.* I used to love getting out on that trail. But this was the first time in a long time."

"I'm glad you took me, before I left. That was a lot more scenic than my route through town."

"When are you leaving?"

"Soon, I suppose."

Ken got up from the couch and walked into the kitchen. He called back to me, "Would you like something?"

I was thirsty. So I got up and joined him in the kitchen. He was standing next to the sink chugging a glass of water. I got a glass from the cupboard and playfully nudged him with my hip so I could get to the tap.

He turned and put his arms around me from behind, put his scratchy cheek on mine and said, "I don't want you to leave."

His touch felt electric, a sensation I had never felt before. I turned around to face him and he kissed me. Really kissed me.

I kissed him back. "I don't want to leave either."

Ken took my hand and led me upstairs.

34

The next morning, I got up first. Went downstairs to make a pot of coffee. God, I needed coffee. What a night! I felt sore all over, achy, whisker burned ... in short, glorious.

I heard a familiar thud, thud. Here comes lover boy.

"Good morning," Ken said sheepishly.

"Good morning to you. Coffee?"

"Damn right."

We sat quietly at the kitchen table, waking up and enjoying the coffee.

Outside a car door slammed. A few seconds later we heard clomping up the porch steps. I got up first to answer the door, but it swung open before I got there.

In walked a beautiful, perfectly groomed flower child with long blond hair held in place by a headband. She wore leather sandals, floor-length sundress, an open suede jacket with fringed pockets, braided leather belt tied in front, a smaller version of Ken's peace sign necklace, and a daisy tucked above her ear. Who does that? Where do you even find a daisy? I hate her already

I saw my reflection in the window of the door when I closed it behind her. Oh God. My hair stuck straight up and out on the left side. I looked like Clarabelle in a sweat suit.

Standing next to her in the kitchen I asked, "Who are you?" I'm sure that sounded awful.

"Laci, with an "I", who are you?"

But before I could answer came, "Oh, hi Laci. Been awhile. Come on in," chimed Ken from behind me.

"Hi sweetie. Who's your *friend*?" Laci said, as she kissed Ken's cheek.

"I'm Willa. Nice to meet you," I lied.

"I didn't think you'd be back," Ken said.

"I came back to pick up some things I left, and to see how you're doing," flower girl said.

"I'm doin' fine, Laci. How about you?" Ken said.

"Can I talk to you outside for a minute?" she said.

"That's cool. Let me change out of my sweat pants," Ken said.

Ken ran back upstairs. "So how do you know Ken?" Laci asked.

"Mutual friend. How about you?"

"Oh, I've known Ken *forever*. We bought this farm years ago to get away from the military-industrial war mongers."

"Why'd you leave?"

"It got weird. This place started to freak us all out. But I'm back now."

"Okay, let's take a walk, Laci," Ken said on his way back down the stairs.

35

Ken opened the door for flower girl and out they went.
Now what? His *chick* suddenly shows up. "Oh, I'm
back now," really flower child. They've been gone a long time.
What the hell are they talking about? Me? Getting back together? Shit, I hate this. I better pack up, this is too nerve
wracking and I have to get home anyway. No reason to stick
around for their little commune reunion. Let me see what
they're up to first. I peeked out the front window. They're
near the big stump facing each other. She's taking his hand.
She put it on her boob! What a whore! Oh, I should talk.
Here I sit after ... well, after.

I'd better go. It won't take me long to pack my overnight
bag. I went upstairs, folded the sweat suit and put it back
on the sink. Wait a minute. The sweat suit ... it's gotta be
flower child's. I was wearing *her* clothes. This is too much. I
rushed downstairs to make my escape, but ran smack into
"Laci with an I," coming back into the kitchen. She looked
pissed. Don't worry, I'm leaving.

She went upstairs without saying anything to me.

"Ken?"

"I'm out here."

I joined Ken on the porch. "I've got to get going. You probably need some space now and I'm kind of intruding on a
private matter."

"Are you talking about Laci? Look, I realize having her

pop in like this seems weird. But she's just here to pick up some of her stuff she left."

"It didn't look weird when you were ... talking."

Laci pushed through the door carrying a pair of shoes, an umbrella, and an armful of clothes. She walked quickly past, but stopped on the steps, turned around, and looked directly at me, "You can keep the sweat suit," and she was off.

"She didn't look very happy," I said, with as much sarcasm as I could muster.

"Very perceptive," Ken said, mimicking my tone. "She wanted to move back in. But not with you here. I kind of told her you were here now and weren't going anywhere. That was a deal breaker for her. I hope what I said is true."

"So you're trading *chicks?*"

"Let's call it an upgrade."

"You're so crass," I said.

"Wait a minute. I think you may have traded one douche bag for a fine, burned-out hippie artist. That's an upgrade in my book," Ken said.

"Mine too."

36

I got a letter back from the Secretary of National Museums of Canada Corporation co-signed by a representative of the newly established Canadian Archeological Association. They're interested in re-patriating François, had followed up with the coroner, and thanked me for the information I sent. They would apprise me of the outcome.

François' future was moving along a little faster than mine. I wasn't able to sublease my apartment in Madison, but that may have turned out okay. Despite the B+ Dan gave me for the semester, I was invited back for the second year. I'm not going to pursue it now. Still have a sour taste.

In early September I met with Dan at his office. We had a nice talk, he even got me a job working in the primate lab. It was easier seeing him than I thought it would be. Dan seemed happy to hear I was better, but I could tell he was skeptical. I guess he figures once a wacko always a wacko. Talking with him again made me realize that I had been trying so hard to be the pretty, demure, deferential girlfriend I thought he wanted that I couldn't be myself. It seemed like my job was to practice for a role and prepare for being "on stage" whenever we went out. It was stressful, especially when I needed his reassurance during my struggle. He couldn't give that to me. Once my visions started, I was a nervous wreck and an embarrassment to him.

It feels so different when I'm with Ken. It's not work, it's fun to be with him. We laugh all the time. I don't have to try to be anybody else. He even likes the "pushy broad."

I enrolled in the School of Education. Turns out I only need a Methods class and student teaching to qualify for my teaching license. The "baby boom" has schools being built everywhere, and of course a need for new teachers to staff the schools. I would be licensed to teach broad-field social studies, psychology, or sociology in a high school. That would be fun and I shouldn't have any trouble getting a job when I graduate in May. I could start teaching somewhere next fall.

Ken even said that he would consider teaching art if he were able to resolve the draft issue by the end of the year. When he told me that, my jaw hit the floor. "What about that 'I hate kids' thing," I asked him. Well it turns out he has problems with "ankle biters," which he clarified meant elementary-age children. He thinks he could enjoy teaching high school art. He applied for second semester and if accepted at UW, he may move in with me in Madison, if everything goes well.

He said he sold the last of his farm crop to Bud and Kathy who visited a week ago. Ken isn't going to replant, and instead has listed the farm for sale. He will split the proceeds with Laci and Scot, two of the members of the original group who lived at the farm and put money into the purchase. Laci's dad is a pediatrician in Schaumberg. Ken said she had a pretty good-sized trust fund at Dean Witter and tapped into it to help buy the farm. I don't feel so guilty about keeping her sweat suit anymore.

When I'm in Madison and he's in Galesville, I really miss him. I think he misses me, too. It's hard to believe we have known each other less than four months. It seems like it's been years. We click. He makes me laugh, and cleans up really well. I'm looking forward to having him meet my family on Thanksgiving. I think Mom is going to be disappointed this time. She adored Dan. Dad, I'm not so sure. If anybody thinks for himself, it's Ken. He has an opinion on everything.

Generally, keeps it to himself, but if you ask what he thinks, watch out, Dad.

Ken has been painting again. I don't know much about art, but I like what he paints. I'm biased, of course. Most of his works are abstracts, but when he tells me what it represents or what he's trying to convey, I can see it. He whitewashed over some of the canvases on which he painted his nightmares, and burned the most painful of his "Frenchie pictures." I asked him if I could have the painting of Shiree and the one with the autumn leaves and tree trunk that led us to the basswood in his front yard. I wanted some remembrance, and he was happy to give the paintings to me. Other than an occasional emotionally benign dream about finding François and seeing him protruding from the stump, there haven't been any nightmares, visions, obsessions, sleep deprivation, depression, delusions, or sudden onset of memories. Ken hasn't had any of those symptoms either.

37

Early on Thanksgiving morning, I drove back to Galesville to pick up Ken and take him home to meet my family. Galesville is on the way home from Madison, so I turned down his offer to drive. When I got there, a car with United Farm Agency painted on the side was pulling out of the driveway. Ken told me the realtor dropped off an offer from a buyer interested in the farm. Ken said it was a good offer and thought he should call Laci and Scot to apprise them right away. We went to the diner to use the phone and had a late breakfast.

Scot wasn't home, but his roommate told Ken he'd pass the message on to Scot when he got back from work. Laci answered when Ken called. The conversation was a lot longer than I thought it should be. When Ken got back, he could tell I was interested in the conversation, although I didn't ask. It seemed Laci might be a pain in the ass over the sale. She said she doesn't want to sell and is still considering moving back whether I'm there or not.

You've got to give her points for persistence. Ken said he wasn't too concerned because Laci tends to be a bit of a drama queen and will probably accept the deal after her obligatory period of whining expired. He was sure Scot would agree to the deal. They will each make a profit and Scot needs the money. In fact, Scot asked Ken to sell the farm or buy him out last year, right after he left.

While we ate our breakfast we got caught up. Ken decided that the strategy he and my brother Peter had discussed was his best choice of the "shitty or shittier" options he had on the draft. He sent a letter to his draft board in Minnesota with his new address informing them he was registered in Wisconsin since he hadn't heard anything from Minnesota. Two weeks before, he drove to Eau Claire to register. When he did, they admonished him for his negligence and told him he was eligible for this year's draft and his name was immediately entered. There were no other repercussions, but no turning back either. Ken was shocked to hear that they were already drafting guys with lottery numbers up to eighty-one. They were only in the sixties a few weeks earlier. His eligibility would last until December 31, of this year, 1971. By the end of the year, he will know whether he is going to be drafted or not. That will happen if they draft up to or past the number ninety-seven. If not, his obligation to participate in the draft will be met and he can go on peacefully with his life.

I told Ken about my conversation with Dan and that Dan even helped me get a job at the primate lab, mostly cleaning out rhesus monkey cages. Ken joked that I just took the job for the glamour, but we both knew I needed the income. I owed Mom and Dad money, had burned through most of my savings, and had to pay for my apartment. As long as I reenrolled at UW, I won't need to make payments on my student loan, at least.

38

We arrived at my parent's house in the middle of the afternoon on Thanksgiving Day. The driveway already had three cars parked there—both of my brothers and it looked like Uncle Michael and Aunt Anna. I loved them both. They were so easy to talk to, positive and always supportive. Their kids were a little spoiled, but I guess I'm not one to talk.

We pulled in behind Peter's car. Before we got out, I asked Ken if he was ready.

"You ask me that like we're about to charge the enemy. They're not the enemy, right?"

"No, they're not. Actually, I think you'll like them and I know you will fit right in. It's just that meeting the 'parents' can be disconcerting. Are you nervous?"

"Maybe a little. But after the year I just had, I think I can handle your family."

"Good. Okay, charge!"

Mom answered the door and immediately called Ken, Dan. Embarrassed, she corrected herself. Ken took it pretty good-naturedly. I introduced Ken to everyone. Peter came over and began talking with Ken about the news of the day—D. B. Cooper hi-jacking a plane and bailing out with $200,000. When the conversation turned to the draft and basswood logs, I figured Ken was in good hands, so I walked into the kitchen to help Mom, Joanie, and Pete's wife, Lynn, get dinner ready. It was nice to get caught up with the girls in the family. I didn't know Lynn very well, met her two or three times before their wedding last year, but Joanie was like a sister. We're about the same age and used to see each other regularly before she had kids.

Once it seemed that Mom had everything under control in the kitchen, I went to find Ken to make sure he was comfortable. Dad had joined the conversation with Pete and Ken after he had gotten Ken a drink. They were all laughing hard about something. I wasn't sure I wanted to know what it was, so I approached cautiously. Evidently, at different times they had all been to the same bar across the river from Red Wing that served breaded turtle. They were laughing over their shared recollection of an old newspaper article framed and displayed next to the bar that showed a picture of a huge dead snapping turtle. It had been snared in fishing nets nearby. The turtle's mouth was propped open and a man had placed his head in the opening to give a perspective of the size of the beast.

"Sorry I missed that excursion," I said sarcastically.

"It was a real classy place. You might not have felt comfortable there," Peter chided.

I was happy to see that Ken seemed genuinely to be enjoying himself with my family. I could tell Dad liked him right away and Pete already knew him. Dad was clearly relieved I wasn't having visions and nightmares anymore. He was supportive throughout my psychological struggles, but I think he was more concerned than he let on.

While we were setting the table, Joanie and Lynn must have told me a half dozen times how handsome Ken was. Yeah, I thought so too. When I checked in with the boys again, they were talking about Ken's draft status. The lottery was up to eighty-four already. Despite attempts by Pete to be positive, Ken was really concerned; after all, the US and South Vietnam had just invaded Laos. To my surprise, he said that if his number was called, he would go. I'd have bet the farm that he would head to Canada or try to go off the radar again.

"You would go into the army if you were drafted?" I asked, just to be sure I understood what he said.

"Yup. I have to get my draft status resolved one way or another. I don't want to be hiding the rest of my life, and don't want to put you through that either, Willa. Besides, if I don't go, some other guy, who doesn't want to go any more than I do, will have to go in my place, and that's the only way I will get my parents to talk to me again. But it's going to be a nerve-wracking five weeks. I can't believe they're already calling lottery numbers in the eighties. I'm preparing myself mentally to the possibility of going to 'Nam."

My Dad asked him what he thought about fighting the war in Vietnam. This was a topic I was sure would trigger one of Ken's diatribes, and it did.

"Why the hell fight in Southeast Asia? The leaders of South Vietnam are just a bunch of corrupt, inept fools. They're only in power because we keep them there. Who are we kidding? That's democracy? We have the best equipment, planes, ships, artillery, all that stuff. But some twelve-year-old Gook with a rifle hiding in the jungle is just as deadly as a trained, fully-equipped GI. So what do our geniuses say, 'Oh let's just defoliate the whole frickin' jungle.' So North Vietnam just moves their supply lines to Cambodia and Laos or into tunnels. It's a war of attrition and we're going to lose, despite spending billions and losing tens of thousands of our kids." Ken stopped, I think to gauge how much damage he might have done.

"You'd just let one country after another in Southeast Asia go communist?" Dad asked.

"Hell yes. If the people of South Vietnam, Burma, Laos, all of 'em want to fight communists, great. Look how expensive that will be for the North and China to try to quell rebellion in four or five different countries at the same time. Let them fight against guerillas in the jungle, not us. Taking that territory will only sap China's economy and make them more vulnerable if they try to expand. We've got the best navy, best air force, best soldiers. Let China try to take the Philippines, Taiwan, or go into Pakistan or India where any of those countries can throw a million-man army into the field. That's when and where we fight. Not where the Chinese pick."

"So why are we there then? Hasn't anyone in the government figured that out?" Dad asked.

"None of them have the balls to take a position other than self-serving political posturing. They all want to say, 'I'm the toughest on communism.' 'No I am the toughest.' Rhetoric is easy. War is even good for our economy. The only way they'll get the message is if the kids that are supposed to bail the assholes out by going over there to fight say 'hell no we won't go.' Now that the voting age is eighteen, we can vote those assholes out. Why fight a war we can't win? Fight for the right reasons, fight for a country with leaders that want democracy, but not just for political expediency or communist paranoia."

"But you're willing to go in. Isn't that a little hypocritical?" Dad asked.

"It is. This is a hard decision. As much as I hate the war, I hate the notion of going through life as a fugitive and estranged from my family even more. It's that simple."

"Enough politics!" I said.

"Dinner's ready, let's eat," Joanie called.

39

That was the most fun I've had at Thanksgiving in a long time. I generally avoided bringing someone because it was inevitably stressful, awkward, and painful. I would fret over how I looked. What was my boyfriend thinking? What were my parents thinking about my boyfriend? That didn't happen with Ken. He was just being Ken. A cleaned-up version of Ken, at ease and able to talk with anyone and everyone.

As disappointed as my mom was that Ken wasn't Dan, she seemed to warm up as the day went on, even hugged him when we left.

When I talked to Dad after Thanksgiving, he said he saw a lot of himself in Ken— stubborn independence. He said that World War II was different and he felt good about enlisting, but if he were in his twenties now, his view of the Vietnam War and the protesting probably would have been the same as Ken's.

I could tell Mike and Peter both liked him.

40

Ken called to tell me the deal went through on the sale of the farm and he hoped he could stay with me in Madison for a while. I was delighted to have him move in. He must have assumed I would agree because he showed up two hours later. His beater of a pickup was piled high with his stuff, tied down with the clothesline he had used to hang his crop to dry in the barn. He looked like an Okie out of a Steinbeck novel. I didn't realize how much I missed seeing him, and ran out to greet him with my biggest bear hug.

We started to unload. Easels, canvas, four boxes of books, one box of clothes, kitchen table with three chairs, nightstand, one end table, bed frame with spring and mattress, and oh no, under it all—that smelly, lumpy old couch!

"Ken, the couch?"

"I wasn't sure and didn't want to be presumptive about my quarters. So, I threw it in."

"How about if we throw it *out*. Please, let's just leave it here next to the sidewalk. Some students will come by and pick it up, it'll be gone by morning."

"I thought you liked that old couch?"

"Ah, no."

We finished unloading his stuff, the couch secure on the curb. I showed him where to park and then gave him a tour of my apartment. Three rooms including the bedroom, kitchen, and the "spacious" 10 x 15-foot combination, living room, library, office, and foyer. Ken's stuff was piled just inside the door.

"It's a nice place," Ken said.

It's a dump, and I assumed Ken was being facetious.

"Yeah, a real palace."

"No, I really like it. But it seems smaller than you described it. I see what you mean about the couch."

Maybe compared to that farmhouse he's been living in, this apartment looks decent. It is a hell of a lot cleaner.

"It looks a little smaller with a truck load of stuff in the entry, and the couch is on the curb not because there isn't room, but because I still haven't gotten that smell out of my head from when I slept on it."

"Yeah, I know. Look Willa, if my being here is going to be a pain, I can look for a place of my own if you prefer."

"I don't prefer. I really want you here, Ken. We'll make do."

"Good, and I'll kick in for rent." Ken reached in his shirt pocket and pulled out a check and showed it to me—$7,200.

"We almost doubled our money in two-and-a-half years. Even Laci has finally admitted she was happy with the deal. So, if I get drafted I won't be here past the first of the year. If not, I've got enough money to pay for another semester or two, if I need it to get my teaching certification and to pay rent. I wouldn't have come here if I was going to freeload."

We got caught up on the draft, which of course was on the top of Ken's mind. With less than three weeks till the end of the year they were drafting all the way up to number ninety. It was going to be close. He decided that he would try to enroll starting with the second semester in mid-January, if he can get in. If he was drafted, he could get his tuition money back. Ken seemed to relax some after we changed the subject. I offered to take him on a walking tour of campus. He agreed and asked if we could go through the primate lab. Ken said he wanted to see where I worked and was interested in the research going on there.

When we got to the lab, Ken showed a lot more interest

in the rhesus monkeys than my job there. I took Ken to the corner of the lab where my favorite monkey "Spiro" was. Spiro screamed excitedly as he usually did when I came to see him. I went to the fridge and came back with Spiro's favorite treat, three grapes. I warned Ken, "Spiro likes to bite."

Spiro scrambled over to the side of the cage to grab his snack. I let him scoop the grapes out of the palm of my hand. After gobbling them down he reached out through the cage, grasped and gently held two of my fingers. Ignoring my warning, Ken put his hand through the cage as far as he could to scratch Spiro's chin and ear. To my amazement, Spiro tilted his head back seeming to enjoy being scratched.

"Spiro never lets strangers touch him! I suppose the next thing you'll want to do is go inside the cage to pick ticks and groom each other."

"No thanks, I'm good. But I sure could use some dinner. And after dinner, let's see a movie," Ken suggested.

"I'm hungry, too. What movie do you want to see?"

"Let me surprise you."

We stopped for cheeseburgers and a beer on State Street. After we finished, Ken led the way toward the theater near the capitol.

"I saw the marquee when I drove past it on the way to your apartment this afternoon and knew we had to see it," he said.

"Well, what is it?"

"You'll see soon enough."

About half a block away I could only read "Starring Gene Hackman." A few more steps and I was able to read the front of the marquee, *The French Connection.*

"How apropos!" I laughed.

"I thought so too, and it's supposed to be good."

41

With classes out for Christmas break I didn't have any trouble finding someone to cover my hours at the primate lab. Ken didn't have plans or any place to go for Christmas and accepted my invitation to spend a few days over the holidays at my parent's house. I thought I'd better call my mom to be sure that was all right. It was. Mom said Ken could stay in the boy's old room, adding very Mommishly, "I don't have any control over what you two do in Madison, but I do here."

"Okay Mom."

Ken and I drove up a day later than we had planned because a snowstorm dumped six inches of snow in Madison and ten inches up north. There were a few slippery spots, but we arrived early in the afternoon on Christmas Eve. When we walked in, Dad, Pete, and Mike were talking about how miserable the Packers were this year. There was some football game on, but they didn't seem to be watching. They all stood up, "Merry Christmas," shook hands with Ken, and hugged me hello. Ken and I joined them. I thought I'd sit for a while with Ken before I went into the kitchen to help Mom.

"The Packers only won four games all year!" Pete said.

"We got spoiled by Lombardi. For that last eight or ten years they were one of the top two or three teams in the league. Now it's Miami. Hell, they blew the Pack out last week. I turned it off, I was so disgusted. What was the score, thirty to three?" Dad said.

"It wasn't quite that bad, twenty-seven to six," Ken said.

"That's right. Oh, by the way Ken, how are you doing with the draft?" Mike asked.

"So far so good, but they are getting so damn close, I'm losing hope," Ken said.

"You still considering going in if your number is called?" Pete asked.

"Yeah. But it's just nerve-wracking watching and waiting, not being able to do anything until I know one way or the other."

Lynn came into the living room. "Merry Christmas, Ken; Merry Christmas, Willa. Willa, can I rescue you from the guys? They've been commiserating about the Packers all afternoon. Come in the kitchen and have a glass of wine. Joanie and Mom could use some help with the ham."

I caught everyone up on my plans and Ken's situation. Joanie nudged me a couple of times when we were talking about Ken. I think her message was "Well are you two getting serious?" But she didn't say it.

Dad hurried into the kitchen a minute later and went to the fridge, got four beers, winked at me and left.

Little Anna was fussing, and Joanie handed her to me. "You may want some practice."

Epilogue

On December 31, 1971, the final draft number was read: ninety-five. Ken and I were watching the news when it was announced. Ken's number was ninety-seven. He was not going to be drafted. We celebrated ... a lot. What a relief! This was the best lottery we could have possibly won!

We were both enrolled in the College of Education at UW starting mid-January. Before the semester began, Ken took me to meet his parents in Edina. His father, Butch, was nearly as tall as Ken, but with something of a beer gut—almost covered by an "America, Love it or Leave it" t-shirt. Despite the fact that Ken made himself eligible for the draft, albeit reluctantly, Butch was very cool, no hug, not even a handshake. He just half-heartedly waved. I thought the description Ken gave of his dad on our drive to Edina was an exaggerated caricature. It wasn't. Even had the same boot camp crew cut. I tried not to stare at it. His hairline sunk nearly halfway down his forehead and his hair was cut so short that it exposed an incredible combination of cranial nooks, ridges, and bumps, enough to keep a phrenologist busy for hours. His perpetual frown and low brow reminded me of a bulldog.

Ken's mother, Ellie, was a thin, graying brunette, "bob" hairstyle, and attractive. She reminded me of a slightly smaller and older Jackie Kennedy. Ellie could not contain her unmitigated joy at seeing her son again after three years. She gushed and hugged, unaware of or simply ignoring the icy stare of her husband's disapproval. At five foot, maybe five-one, she had to stand on her tiptoes to get her arms around Ken's neck, even with him bending forward. She hugged me, too, and reflexively patted the side of my face. She said she couldn't remember seeing Ken so happy, which she attributed to me. She led us to the living room and offered us tea or beer. Ken declined a beer, but I took her up on her tea offer, which seemed to delight her.

Ken and I sat next to each other on the couch. After returning with two cups of tea, Ellie took a seat across from us in the straight-backed padded chair. We both set our tea on the coffee table between us. She gestured to Ken's father to take what I assume was his usual spot, the oversized recliner next to her. Instead, he stayed in a rocking chair on the other side of the room, put his bottle of Schlitz on a sewing table next to him, and crossed his arms. After an hour, Ellie finally ran out of questions to ask Ken and me, and the conversation waned. Ken's father hadn't said a word the entire time until he said something, but it sounded more like a grunt. I believe he had made an offer to get anyone who wanted one a beer. There were no takers, and he resumed his spot after returning with one for himself. After Ken got caught up on how his sister Kathy was doing, and heard some news his mother had gleaned from the moms of a couple of his high school buddies who she sees in church, Ken announced it was time for us to leave. We had a long drive ahead of us.

Hugs all around from Ellie. Butch shook Ken's hand after Ken walked over to him and put his out. I warranted a goodbye wave from Butch.

On the drive back to Madison, Ken said he thought the visit went as well as he could have hoped. Maybe better. It would take some time, but he was confident that each successive visit would be easier. His dad would eventually get acclimated to the idea that his son was going to be his own man, and that like it or not we very well may be the parents of his grandchildren someday. I didn't sense much warming by Butch toward me, but his mother more than made up for it. She couldn't have been more gracious. Despite the size difference, I saw a lot more of Ken in his mother than his father, not just in the resemblance, but their mannerisms, facial expressions, and sense of humor. In fact, it is hard for me to believe Ken and Butch were even related.

By April, Ken and I began applying for teaching positions. We interviewed in May. By the end of June, we each had a contract to begin teaching in the fall at the new high school in Eau Claire. Ken would teach art and be an assistant track coach, I would teach psychology and sociology. Before school started in September, we got married.

Despite his "I hate kids" comment, Ken seemed to have found his calling. All the kids loved Mr. Ludwig. I think he was having fun with art for the first time in a long while. He might have liked the attention, too. He was painting again in his "deKooning" style and actually selling some of his stuff.

At first, I really enjoyed the challenge of a new career and loved working with the kids. But after the second year I felt a redundancy to presenting the same material three or four times a day and then starting over again the next semester. Sure, the smiling faces changed, but the challenge was dissipating. For really dedicated teachers that doesn't happen, so I discovered I wasn't one.

Ken and I were delighted when I got pregnant that fall. I taught through the school year but resigned after little Billy was born. I became a stay-at-home mom. Ken was able to get his Master's Degree in art over two summers, which bumped up his salary. With the occasional income from selling a painting or two, and working with a couple of other teachers doing landscaping over the summer, we were able to buy a house. I planned to go back to work after Billy started school, but deep down I hoped I wouldn't. I really loved being a mother and didn't want to miss anything during Billy's first few years. Besides, we wanted at least one more child, hopefully a little girl.

Five weeks before Billy's first birthday, Ken had him

laughing so hard it made Ken and I laugh too. Ken was playing Billy's favorite game "get mom!" Ken would hold Billy against his chest facing out and say "let's get mom!" and run after me. I, of course, was supposed to escape from them. Billy would laugh hysterically the whole time! He never seemed to tire of that game. If it wasn't so damn cute, I would have been happy to redirect Billy to something that required less chasing around on my part, but didn't have the heart.

After a longer than usual pursuit, Ken and I sat down breathing heavily, Billy was still laughing, chatting up a storm with his "almost words" and cooing at Ken.

I looked at Ken and smiled. Smiling back, Ken said, "You know what?"

"What?"

"If it wasn't for François there wouldn't have been us or Billy. I'd probably still be an unemployed hippie draft dodger, or in jail now," Ken said.

"Yeah, and I'd probably be a newly-minted Doctor Heinlein and married to boy genius, doing something I really didn't want to do, with someone I didn't want to do it with."

"Thank you, François," Ken said.

"Yup, thanks François," I agreed.

Did I just hear Billy say "*de rien*"?

218